PRAISE FOR
HAUNTED ECOLOGIES

"These ecological horror stories are fueled by melancholy, anger, grief, and an abiding tenderness both toward the damaged world and toward ourselves... It's an excellent book and I want you to read it."—Nathan Ballingrud, author of *Crypt of the Moon Spider* and *The Strange*

"A startlingly bright collection of sparse and spooky ecological horror stories" —*Library Journal*

"These stories are indeed haunted places - full of mist and smoke and monsters and shadows but above all, the mess that makes up the human race. And they're going to stay with me for a long time." — Amber Sparks, author of *And I Do Not Forgive You*

"The intricate eco-horrors of *Haunted Ecologies* skillfully thread the needle between sorrow and transformation, between collapse and survival. These stories are steeped with regret for the choices that we've made, but Farrenkopf still throws us a lifeline—the possibility that something will survive, even if it's monstrous, even if it costs us." —Nadia Bulkin, author of *She Said Destroy*

"*Haunted Ecologies* is a collection written in a classic and melancholic voice, filled with a blend of cli-fi and academia that follows enduring families, illuminating collapsing economics and ecosystems, presenting readers with nature metaphors that symbolize the change, turbulence, and turmoil in human lives. At the core theme of these interconnected short stories is the criticism of corporate corruption, wasting landscapes that offer daunting and prophetic futures, continuing memories, things lost and changed through translation, yet it also offers hope, even with the looming end of the world." —Ai Jiang, Bram Stoker and Nebula Award-winning author of *Linghun*

HAUNTED ECOLOGIES

A SHORT STORY COLLECTION

COREY FARRENKOPF

JOURNALSTONE
YOUR LINK TO ARTIST TALENT

ISBN: 978-1-68510-140-4 (trade paper)
ISBN: 978-1-68510-141-1 (ebook)
Library of Congress Catalog Number: 2024947263

First printing edition: February 14, 2025
Printed by JournalStone Publishing in the United States of America.
Cover Artwork: Mikio Murakami
Edited by Sean Leonard
Proofreading, Cover Layout, & Interior Layout by Scarlett R. Algee
Author photo by Gabrielle Griffis

JournalStone Publishing
1400 North Wood Rd.
Murphysboro, IL 62966

JournalStone books may be ordered through booksellers or by contacting:
or
JournalStone | www.journalstone.com

For my mother, Kelly, who taught me to love stories.

And to Gabrielle, who taught me how to write them.

TABLE OF CONTENTS

We've Been in Enough Places to Know
11

Mother's Wolves
14

Translations for a Dead Sea
26

Fences and Full Moons
44

The Tap, Tap, Tap of a Beak
47

The Burnt Floor
61

Wash'ashore Plastics Museum
68

Growth/Decay
79

Exoskeletons
93

Something Aquatic. Something Hungry.
105

Dredging the Bay
110

Green Thought
126

The Man of Reeds and Seaweed
140

To Tend a Grove
147

Waterlogged
175

Publication Credits

Acknowledgments

About the Author

HAUNTED
ECOLOGIES

WE'VE BEEN IN ENOUGH PLACES TO KNOW

The condos' septic failed. It was among the deficiencies that developed over the first two years of habitation. The paint job peeled around month two. The cellar's cement walls cracked after month six. The HVAC system coughed acrid black smoke on the first cold day in November. The list went on, but the septic was what forced inhabitants out, what prompted the lawsuits over the shoddy construction, forged permits, and the outrageous price residents paid to inhabit the crumbling beachside villa.

The building had begun to lean toward the bay. High tide lapped through backyard decking, dragging the seawall away, speeding erosion. A red X was painted across the front door, situated between two boarded-up windows that Glen knew were Tiffany glass. He'd snapped cell-phone shots of the ornate panes from within to show his girlfriend how misplaced the builder's priorities were.

Glen worked for SeaSide Property Management. Twice a week, he walked through each condo looking for squatters. The owner believed he could salvage his business venture before the structure descended into the sea. Glen had his doubts, considering the amount of water in the basement and the veins of mold beneath the peeled paint. Then there was the thing swimming in the basement, drifting between steel Lally columns, the ridge of knotted spine pressing up through the water.

Glen's boss said, *If it's not kids or homeless sleeping in there, best not mention it to the cops.*

Every time Glen walked through the sagging halls, he considered more appropriate land usage. The 6.2 acres could have been left as protected wetland, breeding grounds for waterfowl, a sandy stretch of beach for turtles to lay their eggs. If it had to be housing, why not affordable housing? Fifteen units at several hundred thousand a pop could have been a hundred affordable units for working-class families.

Glen considered renting rooms to kids he went to high school with who griped about the housing shortage online. No one would know. He was the only employee checking the building. It would be easy to forge requests to have the power turned on. The septic only leached a negligible amount of fecal matter into the surrounding waters.

But Glen couldn't do it. Beyond the environmental sin, the building was going to fall into the sea. He wouldn't let even vague acquaintances drown in their beds.

There was also the creature living in the basement and its waterlogged birdcalls gurgling at all hours of the night. Glen didn't know how it would take to having neighbors.

Glen only had to flash his pistol twice. Most squatters left peacefully once discovered. The first was a pair of heroin addicts shooting up in a second-story unit. The second was a man kneeling on the basement stairs, screaming at the creature below. The thing had grown restless, whipping the standing water into a froth, its three skeletal tails cracking against the sunken steps in abrasive rasps. It nosed out of the water, a collection of mouths and overlapping teeth worrying the air, biting down again and again on its own scaled flesh. Glen had grown protective of the aquatic being, so he was a little more gruff with the man than he had been with the addicts.

As he threw the man, still ranting, into the street, Glen managed to catch the end of his warning, *That monster will be the death of us, mark my words.* And Glen did. He jotted them down in the weekly report his boss continued to ignore.

Glen had grown lazy in his search for squatters, preferring to stand at the top of the basement stairs, watching the creature's fins as it gracefully swam about. He'd throw food into the water: hot dogs and bread, chocolate bars and cheese sticks. But the creature never ate, its many mouths remaining shut. When the laughter of children filtered through the ceiling one night, he couldn't make up an excuse not to look, even though he hated evicting families.

Shouldering through the condo's door, he found three kids huddled around an electric lantern, reading knock-knock jokes from a library book in the dim light, the mother making sandwiches from Kraft singles.

"I'm sorry, but you have to leave," Glen said.

"I know," the mother answered. "Could we just stay the night? The rain's so heavy and there's nowhere to go."

"I want to say yes, but this building's collapsing."

"It won't tonight."

Glenn sighed. "There's also this thing in the basement. I don't know what it eats. You might find it on your doorstep instead of me next time."

"I'm not worried about that. All houses like this have something in the basement, or the attic. Beneath the stairs, under the deck. We've been in enough places to know."

"It's your call. If you promise to be out by morning, I won't call the cops," Glenn said.

"We'll be out before sunrise," the mother replied, resignation tinting her words.

Glenn nodded and walked toward the door. The kids began reading jokes as he slipped around their lantern-lit semicircle. Before stepping into the hall, he turned to the woman. "Do you know what that thing eats? The creature downstairs?"

"I figured it ate whoever lived here first. Why would anyone abandon a house like this otherwise?" the woman said.

"I don't think that's what—" Glen began to say before the woman cut him off.

"No. I'm sure. People don't abandon homes when they actually have them."

Glen nodded, closing the door behind himself. From the woman's wide-eyed look, the way her teeth clenched behind cracked lips, he knew he wouldn't change her mind. The next morning, when he'd come back to check, he hoped he'd find the creature swimming in its usual pool, the condo's walls clean and blood-free, and the children's library books gone from the top floor.

MOTHER'S WOLVES

I pressed *Record* on my mother's cassette deck, the one she had used for the experiment five years before. Leo held the megaphone up, pausing before I gave the signal. We were in a cedar swamp, miles off the main road. A thick weave of branches and brambles choked the air. The usual waterways swimming between moss-laden trees were reduced to a trickle. A dry season sucked up the moisture, allowing us to move between the cedars with ease. The occasional spongy squelch rose beneath our boot heels as we pressed down on the green carpeting. It was a full moon. The wash of pale light made our headlamps useless.

The blank cassette unspooled. A prerecorded howl from a timber wolf barked through Leo's megaphone. It echoed through the trees, shaking sparrows from a nearby perch. With the sound fading, I watched the tape, the red *Record* button flashing. I could feel Leo staring, waiting for my reaction. A minute passed. Then two. Then five. No wolf was going to reply, to prove my theory that yes, they had returned to Maine. I clicked the button off. The whirring tape fell silent. There was a forty-five-minute hike back to my Jeep. We couldn't wait. I had to teach a class at 9 a.m.

"Maybe we should play it one more time?" Leo asked.

"There's no point. If there were another wolf out here, it would have responded," I said, taking out my GPS, its LCD screen aglow.

"They could be shy."

"I don't think you can ascribe human emotions to animals like that—not shyness, at least."

Leo's narrow shoulders slumped as he tucked the megaphone into his backpack. I should have played into his optimism. Leo volunteered five to ten hours a week helping with my study, lugging equipment in and out of dense forests. He was the only undergrad to answer my request for an assistant. He didn't need the extra credit. Every paper he turned in was A-worthy.

Another howl would hurt no one, but the wolf's voice, or lack thereof, hollowed something in my chest. It was the thirty-first night with no reply.

We walked the 1.6 miles through the forest, pushing branches out of our faces, avoiding small pools of murky water. Occasionally Leo would mention some wolf-related trivia. It was a nice gesture, but I knew the statistics. Our outings were part of my thesis. I agreed with him to keep up morale.

"Yeah," I replied, "it's weird how coy wolves are more common than purebred wolves in parts of Canada."

"Apparently they're even on Cape Cod. There's a picture going around the internet of one wading through mudflats," Leo continued, leading into another discussion on gene dispersion and heredity. Even though I craved silence, I was glad to hear that someone else, besides myself, still cared. Leo, despite the evidence, didn't believe wolves were going extinct.

***

The scent of rotting wood and pinesap grew thick while we traversed the flat paths cutting through the underbrush. As the Jeep came into view, I told myself if I didn't catch a response soon, I'd hang up my recording equipment. That, or if I didn't find my mother's lost camp. Whichever came first.

"Mia, what do you think about stopping at the diner before you drop me at the dorms?" Leo asked when we were in the Jeep, tires spitting loose stones. I could tell he had been working himself up to the question. I couldn't crush him. I sensed more than scholarly interest, but a midnight date couldn't happen. The whole stereotype of relationships between grad students and undergrads had historically played itself out. I didn't need to add another page to the book, regardless of the gender swap.

"Not tonight, Leo. I need to figure out what I'm going to teach tomorrow."

"You mean you don't..."

"Nope, I don't plan that far ahead. I have some loose ideas, but that's about it. Don't mention it to the others, right? Our secret." I hoped confidentiality would flatter.

"I would never." He stared out the windshield, face blank, the full moon bathing his angular features and slicked-back hair in pale light.

***

My mother had been part of the first experiment. She wasn't the head scientist of the Wolf Inquiry Project, just one of the more fervent members of the study. Their purpose was to prove wolves had returned to Maine, a state recently abandoned, thanks to temperature hikes, overhunting, and habitat destruction. My mother, along with a team of volunteers, had drifted through the woods around Holden with an identical setup to the one Leo and I now carried. There had been rumors in nearby towns. Several chickens and goats turned up dead and bloody. Ghostly dog-shaped blurs crept across highways. An elderly woman claimed she captured a picture of one on a disposable camera, but the film was too blurry to prove anything.

My mother sent letters, swearing they were close to locating a pack. If found, legislation would be proposed, adding Maine as a sanctuary state to establish a breeding population. The Wolf Inquiry Project took three months. My mother and I usually kept in close contact, but throughout those weeks, I only saw her sporadically. Being apart for so long was a rarity; I had chosen to do my undergraduate at UMaine so I could be close to her. Campus was only three towns away. Mom's brief letters took the place of our weekly Thai-food dates, our trips to the movies, and garden walks.

Their research teams recorded zero howls. On the last day of the study, my mother took a new tape deck out on her own. Many members abandoned the project when no results surfaced. She didn't rendezvous with the scientists at the agreed-upon hour. Nor did she show up the next day. Or the next. She didn't come back at all. Police found her truck on the side of an access road but couldn't locate her body. Every paper said she was dead but published no evidence. I never let their claims of starvation and exposure exist as anything more than hearsay. Statistics said 98 percent of people who go missing in Maine's woods turn up within twenty-four hours. Ninety-nine percent are found eventually. With my mother in the remaining 1 percent, I knew she didn't want to be located. Dead bodies can't consciously evade search teams, grid layouts, German shepherds, and helicopters. I knew she was out there.

Mom had been gone for five years. I wanted so badly to believe I'd find her on the other end of the recorded howls instead of a wolf.

When my father died of a sudden heart attack six years ago, when I was still a senior in college, my mother quit her job as a park ranger in

Acadia and searched for a new cause to throw herself into. Being selected for the research team enabled her to become singularly focused, a temporary reprieve that rapidly morphed into an obsession. With the project's failure and no chance of establishing a breeding population for the wolves, something inside her broke, something that wouldn't let her come back to society and all the reminders that her husband was dead and she hadn't helped the species attain rebirth. With her only remaining distraction gone, it was no surprise she took to the woods. That's what I thought anyway. So I searched, retracing her steps through once-trod forest, picking the same paths and hunting trails she wrote about in letters. I wanted to help the wolves; that part wasn't a fabrication. My advisors hadn't connected our last names. They hadn't considered I'd have an ulterior motive to my studies.

I considered talking to Leo about it, but the intimacy seemed too much and I didn't want to taint his image of what we were trying to accomplish.

***

Like most days, I ghosted through lessons, relying heavily on group discussion. Leo was there, adding his knowledge of dwindling ecosystems to the conversation, comparing statistics of what lived in local forests a hundred years ago to what remained today.

I put a check mark next to every student's name. Full credit for the day, like all days. Between waves of heat pumped through malfunctioning radiators, the throb of fluorescent lights, and the approaching snow clouds, I couldn't drag my mind away from my mother.

During our weekly meeting, my advisor asked if I was sleeping enough. He handed back a typed section of my dissertation. Innumerable red circles and underlined words marred the paper.

"Maybe you should take next semester off, Mia," he said, a hand resting in his thick beard. "If I write you a note, it won't affect your stipend. UNE won't face extinction in your absence."

"I'm fine," I said, paging through the edits. "Long nights out in the woods take their toll after a while, you know?"

"Well, get your sleep schedule in order. No one likes a sloppy scientist." He smiled. "If you change your mind, let me know. We'll work something out."

***

I could feel Leo's eyes as we pushed through the undergrowth of a forest outside Augusta. Part of me knew he was checking out my butt. The other part knew he'd fixated on the revolver strapped to my hip. My advisor said it would be stupid to go that deep into the woods without one. Between bears and moose in rut, who knew what we'd find. A pair of dirt bikers said they came across a wolf-like carcass by a glacial pond. ATV paths crisscrossed the whole wooded region. Their encroachment was illegal, but I appreciated the tip.

"You wouldn't shoot one, right?" Leo asked.

"No way. That would defeat the purpose," I said. "I'd just fire a warning shot. They run at loud noises."

"That makes me feel better." Leo adjusted his glasses with his free hand.

"But if it turns out to be a bear, those things don't scare off easy."

"Let's hope they started hibernation early," Leo said.

"It's about that time."

"As long as they aren't looking for a last snack before the big sleep, we're in the clear," Leo said, raising his arms above his head, clenching his jaw in ursine imitation. I stifled a laugh. We didn't need to spook our quarry.

I looked through the undergrowth for footprints. My mother had small feet. She had been wearing hiking boots with serrated metal treads. I'd recognize them. I always imagined stumbling into a sheltered glade of elms, finding her tent pitched in their shadow; her clothing hung out to dry, a cookfire puffing smoke into the night air. I'd rehearsed my first line: *Professor Folger, I presume.* She loved that Livingstone quote. I'd lead her, half-feral, back to the Jeep, back to my apartment, where she could sleep on my fold-out couch until she reacclimated to society. I had seen documentaries where people fell into hermitic life, how they struggled to reintegrate. That wouldn't be her. Not with my help. I'd file her nails, clean the mud out of her hair, delouse her scalp, remind her she was important, important to me.

I should have known something was wrong when she started writing letters. She had never been all that communicative before. Her words transformed from scant nature observations to an almost cultish devotion to the wolves. She also mentioned Dad a lot. What he would have thought about her work, about the state of the environment. She reminisced about family trips: the time they took me to a Florida alligator preserve and bird sanctuary, how my father taught me the difference between heron and crane, all those hikes to forage for edible mushrooms. She never let me forget how to tell poisonous ones from safe. *Just look under the cap.*

In his youth, before becoming a paper-mill operator, my father had been an animal rights activist. Pictures of him standing next to PETA members, garbed in black, chained before cosmetic factories and redwoods, lined our mantel. That's where my parents met. At a rally against a small, notably abusive zoo fifty miles away from her hometown. Kind of an odd love story, but better than the *I met him on Tinder* line I'd been hearing recently.

***

By the edge of the pond, its crystalline water nearly luminous in the moonlight, we found the corpse of a coyote, ribs protruding through fur, dried blood pulped across nearby trees. A tangle of plastic drifted out of its stomach cavity, along with entrails scavengers left behind. It looked like a trash bag, something that once held a mistaken meal. There was no confusing the coyote for a wolf. Too small, muzzle narrow, the composition of the face, the hue of its fur. I jotted down observations in my notebook and took out the cassette player, a fresh tape in the deck. There was no sense wasting our trip. The terrain matched appropriate habitat. The clean water supply, the proliferation of prey. I had seen rabbit pellets and trees rubbed raw by deer antlers. Roots hung over the pond's edge. There'd be fish in the shallows, waterfowl nesting by the shore.

Leo stood frozen behind me, fearful, staring down at the carcass, oblivious to the equipment I removed.

"Are you with me, buddy?" I asked, shaking the recorder toward him.

"Oh yeah, my bad," he said as he hurriedly drew the megaphone out of his bag, making sure our wolf recording was ready to play from his iPhone.

"You think this will be the time?" he asked.

"I hope so," I said, confident a single reply wouldn't bring my advisors to call off our forest wanderings and abruptly end my search for my mother. They'd want more evidence, not a single fluke.

Leo played the recording once I got the cassette spinning. The howl seemed to grow out of the megaphone, deep and alive, cascading across the surface of the pond to reach the distant shore. Leo looked like he wanted to say something as the sound spread around us, but I held up a silencing hand. The tape was spinning. I didn't want to ruin the recording. As always, the moments passed, the silence thick. Nothing stirred. There were no wolves nearby. Coyotes didn't yip in the distance. I cut the recording and flashed Leo the okay.

"I'm sorry we missed them," Leo said as he zipped the megaphone into his pack, as if the wolves had been there the day before and we were lagging. I didn't have the heart to tell him Maine was likely barren. That the old farmers and widowers who responded to my want ads had declining eyesight or worse hearing.

Despite my melancholy, I couldn't deny his genuine kindness. I was sure if I told him about my mother, he'd have the same reaction. *Oh, that's tragic, can I help? I can set up some trail cams around here...*

"No worries," I replied. "It's not like there's anything we can do to drag them into existence. I'm just glad you're still coming with me. Being alone in the woods sucks," I said, imagining my mother's camp, as always, her ranting to herself, fueling the fire, cupping hands around her mouth to howl at the moon.

"I wouldn't bail on you," Leo said.

"Thanks."

"Any chance we could stop at the diner on the way back? Seeing as how there's no class tomorrow?" Leo asked.

It was Friday night. I couldn't recycle excuses.

"Not tonight. The coyote messed with my stomach. I don't think I can eat anything."

***

I remember helping my mother pack. At the moment, the extra gear wasn't surprising. The bedroll, twin lanterns, canned meat, powdered milk, all those changes of clothes. I helped her fold pants so they would fit in neat balls, tucking socks in on themselves until they were minuscule lumps of wool. She'd purchased the tent at a yard sale months before, had me test it with her in the back yard, bending metal ribs through the fabric. We slept out there one night, pointing out constellations, sipping cheap beer.

"That's Lupus," I said, dragging my finger across pinpricks of light.

"You would point that one out," she said, nudging me in the ribs with her elbow while browning a marshmallow over our rusting firepit.

I had moved back into my childhood bedroom after my father died, helping her cook and clean, getting her library books when she couldn't bring herself to leave the house. She had seen the ad for the Wolf Inquiry Project in one of the nature magazines I picked up. I often wondered what might have happened if I had rented her a movie instead. There were so many moments I should have caught on, so many telltales. The constant glances toward the door, the proliferation of hugs, the words of wisdom siphoned from Hallmark proverbs.

***

"Wolves are one of the healthiest signs of an ecosystem. Knowing there is enough food to feed apex predators means things thrive. It means diversification. That's why we've been searching for them. To prove it isn't so bad...that the forest isn't receding, that..." Leo went on, the heat from the classroom drawing sweat across his forehead. I cut him off with a raised hand.

"A hundred percent right," I said, halting him before he said anything that might tie us together in a more intimate knot. "On that note, I think we'll call it a day. Make sure you submit your response papers by midnight Friday."

The mass of students swept past, the scent of fruited cologne and gym sweat a confusing mixture. Leo remained in his seat, mouth open, mid-thought.

"I was really getting it there," he said. "They needed to hear my point."

"I'm not denying that," I said, leaving my podium. "It's just that I want to get out of here soon. We've got a long drive. Can you be ready in two hours?"

"Hell yeah," he replied, shoveling notebooks into his Wildlife Fund backpack.

"I'll pick you up at your dorm."

***

Leo spent the ride expounding on the effects of removing gray wolves from the Endangered Species Act. Two months before, we spent a weekend with several of my colleagues from the Bio department, protesting the possibility outside the statehouse. Leo's picket sign read, *Weapons Aren't for Wolves!* Mine read, *Wolves Belong in the Wild. Not Trophy Rooms*, in red block letters. Only a single reporter from the local newspaper noticed. The image of the two of us raising our signs made the eleventh page of the Sunday paper below an ad for discounted shotgun cartridges. I don't think the editor intended the juxtaposition.

Removing wolves from the Endangered Species Act would ensure they'd be free rein for hunters. The proposition didn't make sense paired with our findings. Maybe in other states, but not ours. The whole thing made me depressed, considering my own doubts in our study and the doubts about my mother. The two coalesced into one globular letdown. I couldn't save her. I couldn't save them. Even though I stood in the same evergreen glades and inland swamps she had, we felt no closer. I knew the wolves were a long shot, but the reports and sightings seemed more surreal and farcical than they had five years before.

We passed through small villages and reclaimed logging towns; our drive to Wilsons Mills took hours. The trees were denser, older, more foreboding than back East. The town was as far west as we could go without hitting New Hampshire. I read a report about a local sighting by the border. If I read it, maybe Mom did too. It would make sense that her migratory patterns mimicked those of her subjects. I could see her, loping into local libraries, hooded, scanning monthly wildlife journals before retreating to her camp in the forest.

We left the Jeep on the side of a dirt road spanned by power lines, the sun setting, the ground wet from recent showers.

"The US Fish and Wildlife Service can't do that," Leo went on. "They've proven Maine would be perfect for reintroducing the species. The habitat is ideal. It's—"

"I know," I said. "But we've got to be quiet. If there's anything out here, it will hear you and hide."

"Got it." Leo tightened the backpack straps over his shoulders. I really admired his dedication, but the overview wasn't necessary. The title of my thesis was literally "The Potential Benefits of Reintroducing Timber Wolves to Eastern Maine."

We followed a muddy ATV track dissecting the forest, avoiding knee-deep puddles and slippery inclines. Pines blackened my periphery. No movement passed between them; dense branches sucked up all light. The smell of sap was thick in the air, the moist rot of moldering leaves lingering beneath. At one point, my headlamp drifted across bear prints embedded in the mud. I adjusted the revolver strapped to my hip. I wanted to go farther, to where I hoped the forest would thin out. That would be the ideal spot for Mom's camp. It would be the easiest place for wolves to stalk prey. The cool night air wicked through my jacket. *A few more hours*, I told myself; then we could turn back.

We did our first recording by a rock outcropping a distance off the path. The wolf call went up; silence returned. We repacked and trekked deeper into the woods, checking the GPS repeatedly so we wouldn't lose our position. A second recording occurred by a freshwater spring, water bubbling up from the placid depths. Natural water sources were a solid bet. Deer and moose frequented the spot. Wolves were fine eating either. The cassette tape unspooled and gathered the stillness of the air. Leo made a joke about drinking from the pool, but I described the symptoms of beaver fever and he leaned back from the water's surface, his face barely above his moonlit reflection.

"Hey, do I need to apologize for nagging about the diner thing?" he asked as we drifted deeper into the forest.

"No, why?" I said, pushing a branch out of my path.

"I just never want to be one of those guys. You know, the creepy ones."

"You're fine. Don't worry. We can talk about it when we get back to the Jeep, but for now we..." My words evaporated as a series of breaking twigs and shushed branches crackled ahead of us. The steps sounded human, mid-sprint, leaves crushed underfoot. I peered through the trees, searching for the shadowed figure, hoping to find my mother's form painted against an elm, hair streaming. The rush of movement built, swelling into something ethereal. I reached into my pack and took out the tape deck, pressing record. If we were going to stumble upon something, I would not miss out. It's what my mother would have done. I wanted her body to leave the cover of the trees, to recognize her scent in the mix of bark and dirt, to feel her hand graze my skin, pulling me close in the embrace I'd longed for since she left.

There was a hand on my hip, then a tug at my belt—the embodiment of my desired hallucination. The tension and sudden jerking confused me until I saw Leo with my revolver. My mother wasn't there.

"What are you—" I asked before the thing lunged into our midst. Leo pushed me out of the way as the creature separated us. My stomach dropped. All the thrills of potential joy fled with the animal's arrival. It was the size and shape of a large dog, fur hanging thick and tangled. I caught a glint of teeth, peaked rows of white enamel, pink gums beneath, lips pulled back. Then there was the muzzle flash, the ricochet of noise swallowing us as the animal bounded off into the woods, ignoring the path, disappearing into the undergrowth. The kick of its pale gray legs separated the greenery, only to blend and dissipate. I wasn't sure if it was a wolf, a coyote, or a feral dog that had escaped from a local hunting camp.

The tape continued to record in my hand, the endless winding of film against reel. I looked down and knew the only sound heard would be the shot, our screams, and the flutter of paws receding into the woods. It was the same as the blurred photographs I received from the old ladies, the vague voicemails from farmers lamenting dead chickens. If it was a wolf, then yes, they lived in Maine. If it wasn't, well...

My mother didn't carry a gun. If she were tracking such things, the same scene might have played out with a different ending. My mind drifted to the almost lycanthropic being I'd imagined her becoming, half-wolf, half-researcher, neither coming back to me, dead or alive. She wouldn't be my Livingstone, the warm body I'd find on my couch after class. I couldn't kid myself anymore.

Leo helped me up out of the pine needles, brushing away the dropped foliage with his hand.

"They serve omelets twenty-four hours a day, right?" I asked.

"What?"

"At the diner. They serve breakfast twenty-four hours a day, yes?"

"Yeah, why?" Leo asked.

"Because we're not going to find what I'm looking for."

"But we just did. If you play the howl, I'm sure you'll get the reply."

"Maybe, but she's not out here."

"Who isn't out here?" Leo asked, as I inserted a new tape into the recorder.

"I'll tell you when we get to the diner. Grab the megaphone," I said.

Leo seemed to shake loose from my ramble, realizing what I asked. I hadn't detached from our shared reality and the thing we sought together. He raised the plastic mouthpiece to the sky when I flicked on the red *Record* button. The howl peeled out of the horn, chasing the creature's fleeting steps through the thick undergrowth. I stared down at the turning film, heart half-frozen as moments slunk on, wind whispering into the microphone. My finger lingered over the *Record* button, ready to depress the nodule, to accept defeat. Then, in the distance, a single cry rose—met by another, then another, the wolves singing in chorus. It seemed to build endlessly, the vocalization of a species' sorrow manifest across miles, churning and churning. When the howls died, Leo and I looked at each other. We stowed our equipment in their respective bags and took off running toward our Jeep.

Not everything was so close to extinction.

TRANSLATIONS FOR A DEAD SEA

Laura struggled to hold a half-dozen nails between her lips. She'd found the hammer under the sink, along with several rudimentary tools her father had used for cabin maintenance. He had never been very handy. She used her knee to balance the plywood, galvanized steel chilling her tongue. Once the wood was aligned over the first window facing the sea, she leaned a shoulder onto the salt-worn surface, pressing it in place as she drove a nail into the casement. The hammer clatter reverberated in light fixtures and summer screens, a metallic chittering not dissimilar to cicadas.

She repeated the process until the graying wood was tacked in place.

The next board waited beneath the deck. Her father had cut each to the exact dimensions of corresponding windows, eight in all. The only window he left unadorned was the leaky, western-facing skylight. Even though the roof wasn't steep, her father hated ladders, so it was left bare to view every winter snow and swelling Nor'easter. The cabin was only meant for three-season habitation, the insulation thin. Everyone in the area boarded up for winter, to keep out storm winds and the freezing spittle rising off the ocean.

"Isn't it a little early to be putting up the boards?" Ray asked from behind her. He was in his early forties, a thick brown beard covering his face, eyes the color of the sea, wardrobe composed of nothing but flannel.

"Definitely not," Laura replied, words struggling around the nails.

"I'd say we have at least a month of good weather ahead. Won't you miss the view?"

Laura didn't know how to answer honestly, so she lied.

"It'll help me concentrate when I'm translating. If I spend too much time looking at the water, I'm going to get nothing done."

"How is the writing going?" Ray asked, moving to her side, steadying the plywood with a callused hand.

Ray lived in one of the large, renovated ranches across the street. He worked as a maintenance man for the stretch of cabins crowding the road, for summer people incapable of fixing toilets or hooking up propane tanks. They'd known each other for years, only growing close after his wife passed, leaving him with their twin daughters and the ever-encroaching sea.

"It's going," Laura replied. "A few more weeks and I'll be pretty close to the end."

"Your dad would have been proud, finishing it up for him like that," Ray said as Laura hammered another nail. She slipped, aim off, spilling a cascade of galvanized steel across the deck from her tool belt. Laura swore as the two bent to retrieve the sharpened metal. She'd heard too many horror stories of thin-soled sneakers and lockjaw to leave the nails for long.

"Who's to say? I don't think he even knew if it *should* be finished," Laura said once the stray nails were gathered.

Ray looked at Laura askew, then shrugged, going back to holding the wood.

"Well, I'm sure he would be," Ray said.

***

Her father's cottage was identical to the fifteen other white clapboard cottages strung along the road in North Truro, one of the towns farthest out on the Atlantic-wrapped peninsula. Neighboring roads repeatedly washed out with sand, blacktop giving way to soft shoulders, desert-like. Sparse forests of scrub pine pressed up to the dunes, the scent of sap always on the air.

Each building was a single story. Turquoise shutters framed windows. Chimneys divided rooflines. Over their shoulders was Cape Cod Bay, a thin stretch of beach on the opposite side of a concrete seawall. When storms rolled in, roiling waves kicked about front steps, the buildings more aquatic than terrestrial. In October, most were abandoned, the seasonal economy come and gone for the year.

Ray said only eccentrics stuck around.

Laura welcomed the epithet. She had a goat tattoo on her collarbone, had given up dying the gray out of her bangs. She used to stitch patches of band names to leather jackets, fixing studs to shoulders. She was getting too old for that, though, she told herself.

Laura had lost her previous lease in Boston when she could no longer afford the rising rent. It was hard to afford anything in the city when you were single, and after an unpleasant divorce in her late twenties, owning her own place always seemed like a distant daydream. The cottage was her only option, the mortgage already paid. All she had to worry about were taxes and insurance. After the prolonged pandemic, her job, like many, had cut hours and gone remote. The cottage got decent Wi-Fi. It was enough to continue her graphic design work, sketching logos for organic juice shacks, crafting tri-folds for some corporation's overpriced healthcare package.

Her job didn't really matter anymore. It paid the bills, kept the heat on, provided enough for takeout twice a week, but little else. It was her nightly task that propelled her days. Her father, an armchair academic after a lifetime of marine biology, had left behind a poetic text he believed held the secret to many things. He had believed the words could provide hope, a tipping point, some great revelation and unveiling. But he also believed the inverse, possibly one of the reasons he hadn't made it through the sheets of paper now piled on Laura's writing desk.

With the boards up, her view was gone, the ocean curtained by plywood, the desk lit only by the warm glow slipping beneath the lampshade. Now the windows only peered at the backside of graying boards, several dark knots like wide eyes gazing back at her while she wrote, fingers tracking through dictionaries, unheard voices muttering in her ear.

She hadn't wanted to cover the glass, but she didn't have many choices.

They'd get in if she didn't provide a barricade. From the noises she had heard, her sunless rooms were a small price to pay to sequester her from what came in the night.

***

Laura had written a pros and cons list for finishing the translation of her father's found poem.

CONS:

There are still a few trees.

Cori and Mark. Diane. Russel and Taraneh. Cashel, Daria, Ralph. Gabrielle.

Art's thriving.

There are still guitars. Concerts every weekend.

All those retired ladies at the conservation trust.

The girls.

Ray.

PROS:

There are only a few trees.

Most people disappoint me.

Most people don't care about other people, or animals, or plants...especially not plants.

Colony collapse disorder.

Rising ocean temps.

The Sixth Extinction.

Death hornets.

Favorite Indian restaurant closed.

***

Laura's father, while being good with words, had never been the best translator, hence the unfinished manuscript and the age-muddled line he believed could be understood in one of two ways:

Once rewritten, all will be calm and well

or

Once rewritten, none shall remember calm that well

Laura looked at it as a fifty-fifty chance. Pleasant improvements or vague unpleasantries? She didn't know the scale, what extent of healing or joy or despair would come from the fractured lines. The way things were going, those were decent odds. Speeding up the apocalypse wasn't a great option, but continuing on the same trajectory would lead to blight, emptiness, and very little potable water. Laura wasn't very good with knives or machetes, so defending the only clean waterhole for miles seemed like a grim prospect. She'd read the emergency reports, the UN's 2029 predictions and warnings. Local governments were already talking about placing water restrictions on communities, about storing surplus runoff in newly constructed holding tanks isolated from the public. It was never too early to think about where your next drink might come from, her father had always said.

The thought was never far from her mind.

***

Her father had bought the crumbling papyrus from an indoor flea market in Maine. He'd found it nestled in a poster tube between a taxidermied armadillo and a glass case containing antique pearl-handled revolvers. It was in Greek, the language of his great-great-grandfather. Laura had sprung for the Rosetta Stone app for the two of them, promising they'd learn in tandem. It was a point of bonding. He hadn't been doing well since her mother passed, and the daily lessons gave them an easy entry point for conversation. Once she became fluent, her father had promised he'd bring her to Athens.

They had been at the translation for four years, moving between a pile of dictionaries and the app, before lung cancer caught him.

Now it was up to her to figure out the words left behind.

***

Once dusk had settled, a resonant thud quivered through the plywood. Laura's eyes left the half-composed paper, drifting to the hammer she'd left on the table by the door. The door itself was the only point of entry to the cabin. She couldn't board it up and still make it to the store when she needed eggs and milk and basic human contact. She had to hope the new twin deadbolts Ray had installed would hold. It had been a strange request to make, needing two, but Ray seemed to understand the fears of a woman living alone.

There was also the unprotected skylight, but the thing (things?) outside seemed to have no skill in climbing, so Laura pushed the second point of entry from her mind. It would have been even weirder to ask Ray to install another latch up there, or some heavy-duty screen, though she knew he'd be more than happy to do it for her. Ray seemed more than happy to do most things for Laura and that made her glad. After her divorce and five years of on-again-off-again online dating, she had begun to wonder if there were any decent guys left out there.

Decent was only one of many words Laura could think of to describe Ray.

Another thud snaked through the boards, followed by the sound of claws dragging along their surface. Something circumnavigated the outside of the cottage, slender fingertips mapping the borders between her life and theirs. She was still trying to figure out if there was more than one. A flock? A gathering? A parliament? Laura didn't know. She'd only caught glints that first night before she put up the boards. Only the teeth stayed with her, the sight of moonlight catching on enamel.

Either each night they grew more determined at forcing their way in, or there were more of them. More claws scraping at boards, more feet/flippers/tails scuffing along the deck. Whenever she made progress on the translation, the clamoring grew worse, as if each new word called to them more persistently.

The real problem was whether they were the hero or the villain of the story. Had they come to stop her from finishing the manuscript, halting her from destroying the world, saving the human race from an endless dark horizon? Or were they something else entirely?

***

Her father's field of study had been mollusks.

"They're nature's healers," he'd once said to Laura over Thai food, a dinner date of broken Greek underway. "Did you know that one oyster can filter fifty gallons of water a day? We've been trying to find a way to use them to clean up waste in the bay."

"I didn't know that," Laura replied, though she had. It was her father's favorite factoid about his work, most of which was too jargon-heavy for her to follow. But the oysters she understood.

The oysters were one of the reasons her father had fallen so hard into the translation. Their shells were growing thin. Ocean acidification ate away at them slowly year after year. If the trend continued, they would eventually become translucent, like pebble ghosts scattered across the floor of the bay. Then a year or two after that, they'd be dead.

"So you want to save the world for oysters?" Laura asked him one night as he hunched over his papers, lamp bleeding green through its banker's shade.

"What's good for oysters, is good for fish, is good for gulls, is good for us. It's all connected."

***

"I think I'm going to blame vandals," Laura said as Ray examined the shreds of plywood heaped beneath the bay-side windows, a harsh tear dividing the top of the wood from the bottom.

Wind was heavy off the water, a salt sting in the air, their skin peppered by sand. A tumbleweed of a hydrangea head rolled into the dunes, the once blue bloom now decaying brown.

Ray picked up the larger half of the plywood, fingers running along the gashed surface.

"Vandals?" he asked. "Would have thought me and the girls would have heard something. I guess the ocean's been pretty rough lately. Hard to hear anything over all those waves."

"Yeah, let's go with vandals. Who else would do this?"

Laura knew very well who would do this.

Or vaguely well.

Or just vaguely.

She hated lying to Ray, but didn't know how else to explain her current circumstances, poetry summoning potential demons and all.

"If the vandal was a tiger, maybe, but we don't have many of them out here," Ray replied. "I chased off a pack of coyotes a few weeks back, but nothing bigger than those guys."

"So, if it wasn't vandals, or tigers, or coyotes, what would you put your money on?" Laura helped him slide a new piece of wood from the back of his truck, hoping that Ray might know more than he was letting on.

"Have you pissed anyone off lately?"

"I haven't talked to anyone besides you and the girls and a few people at the grocery store in the last month. I might've pissed off one of those retired bagging ladies who's never careful with my eggs, but otherwise, nope."

"Do you have a gun?" Ray asked.

Laura almost dropped her end of the plywood.

"Do you think I need one?"

"Whatever ripped this guy down," he said, gesturing toward the scrap wood, "is big. Biggish at least. People in the Outer Cape get eccentric sometimes. Who knows if someone bought an exotic pet and it's been getting out at night. You know, real *Tiger King* shit. That's the only thing I can think of. Would you like a gun? On loan, of course."

"Can you legally give me a gun?"

"Don't worry, cops aren't going to come around to bother you. In the offseason, they're on call, mostly. And if you shoot something, I'll come running and say I did it. Problem solved. It's not like I'm going to miss a gunshot in the middle of the night."

"Is it safe?"

"Of course. Do you think I'd keep guns in the house around the girls otherwise?"

"Well, if that's the case, yes, I'd very much like a gun."

"It's all yours. You sure there's nothing else to tell?" Ray said, pointing to the wood. "I really can't imagine sleeping through all this."

"Earplugs do wonders," Laura replied, unable to meet Ray's eyes, pretty sure he'd never glimpsed what slipped from the sea nightly.

***

Later that night, Laura lay next to Ray beneath the covers of his queen-sized bed, staring out toward her cottage through the open window, waiting for inarticulate shadows to swarm her doorway. She hadn't left her translation inside. She knew better. It rested in her backpack by the bedroom door. A copy of the first page lay on her writing desk back in the cabin, the lure hopefully singing to those amorphous shapes slouching from the sea.

The night was still early, the girls having gone to sleep after an impromptu ping-pong tournament with Laura. They'd fallen into the custom of batting the hollow ball back and forth most evenings, something to unwind after a long day of school (for the girls) and dread (for Laura).

Somehow, Laura and Ray managed to keep their sex quiet, never waking his daughters, for which she was thankful. Ray's work-toned body was slick with sweat beside hers, one damp arm slung around her waist as he snored into their pillows. He had fallen asleep quick. He'd been rebuilding a neighbor's deck all week. She didn't fault him. It was just nice to not be alone for a few hours, to hear someone else's breath besides her own.

Laura's mind tracked to her pros and cons list, all that would be lost if she were wrong, Ray's name down there at the bottom. The girls. She always wrestled with the same issue before sleep. It was only after dark she doubted her purpose, fearful of mistakes, of losing those she loved.

But those she loved would be lost anyway, just on a later date when tides had risen and cannibalism wasn't so frowned upon.

***

Laura thought of the sections as cantos; she'd been obsessed with Dante's *Inferno* when she was an undergrad and always liked to think of section breaks in poetry as such. She knew that wasn't accurate, but who was there to correct her? Ray wasn't the reading type, and the girls hated anything that resembled homework.

According to Laura's calculations, she was on canto twenty-two of thirty.

It went like so:
By the water I have written.
Several days have passed.
They swim far out. Farther than I might swim.
I don't swim.
I fear what I see on the surface.
I fear what lies below.
If there is no name, it doesn't exist.
I fear I will find the words to describe it.
To call it into life, plucked from my head,
dropped at my feet, writhing limbs and teeth.
I'm often tempted to lay down my pen.
To forfeit these lines.
But it is also these lines that keep them in the water.
But it is also these lines that call them ashore.

***

Laura kept the gun within reach. She left the hammer by the door. She'd seen many horror movies; she knew to tuck plenty of weapons away. A crowbar by her bedside, the tire iron from her trunk beneath the pull-out couch, a scaling knife behind the television. Two steps and she could be at any hiding place. She wasn't sure most of the objects would do much against what she'd seen through the cracked plywood, but it was better than nothing.

The night she had spent in Ray's bed, the creatures had left her cabin alone, as if they knew she wasn't inside, as if they knew she wasn't dragging pencil across paper, thumbing through dictionaries for difficult adjectives. Was it the words that called to them or the work that led to the words? Laura hated not knowing, hated the uncertainty of every aspect of her life, both environmentally and romantically speaking. She didn't know if Ray saw her as anything more than a fun hookup, if he imagined they had a future together, if he'd willingly do all the macheteing to keep their joint water supply safe.

She was trying to work up the nerve to ask, but the timing didn't seem right.

Nothing really seemed right anymore.

***

Three days later, the moon hung nearly extinguished above Laura's cabin, a pale sliver in the overshadowed sky. It cast enough light to make out the teeth, the slap of gums, a tongue tasting the air as if premeditating its next meal. The thing (things?) had pulled down one of the boards, wrenching the nails from their tired hold. The creature lingered for a moment before moving to the next window, talon-fin-fingers scrambling at the boards as if it were blind, as if some other sense guided it to her home.

It gave her comfort to think the creatures weren't intelligent. They had the opening, the glass right before them, her soft skin just beyond that. But instead, they moved to the next window, repeating the previous process. Laura promised herself she wouldn't shoot until they broke through, until she could smell their breath, feel the heat on her neck. If she shot now, she'd have to explain the thing's corpse to Ray, and the police, and every gawker who swarmed the cottage once a photo landed online. If that was the case, she'd have to confess what she was doing, and someone more knowledgeable would take it out of her hands. Laura didn't want that.

The translations were the only thing that made her feel close to her father anymore, the only thing that gave her life purpose. Designing Kale Chip flyers for her day job certainly wasn't cutting it.

As Laura dropped to the next line of text, which she roughly translated as *There will be joy once collapse. Different joy, but joy nonetheless,* she felt as if her father's hand pressed her shoulder, cold fingers gripping her collarbone. His negative image reflected in the glass, his thin face and beard tinted gray, translucent. Laura reached her free hand up, to place it on his, but there was only gooseflesh coursing down her neck, the call of the wind rushing outside, the stomp and drag of the creatures' movements across the deck. His face slipped from the glass, dissolving back into the writhing night beyond, back into her insomnia-addled memory.

***

At some point after midnight, Laura heard a splash, something dropping back into the ocean. She had put her pen down moments before and retreated to the mattress, pulling the blankets up around her ears. She prayed sleep would come.

There were only three more pages to translate. Two more cantos.

It wouldn't be long until she knew which version of her father's predictions was true.

***

"Tigers again?" Ray asked.

It was the fourth time he'd helped rehang the plywood. It was December. The Cape was quiet and gray, the sky low, beach grass freezing in the dunes, their brittle skin snapping like tin bells on windy mornings.

"I think of them as cougars, but that's just me. Tigers are expensive. Cougars are the value point big cat," Laura replied, nails under her tongue.

"Don't you think you should winterize the place, move somewhere inland? Maybe the tigers will leave you alone."

Ray had offered to call the police, or animal control, several times. Each time, Laura refused. She couldn't risk interruption to her work, no more than she already added with her visits with him and the girls.

She'd started to hear her father's voice, reading over the lines, suggesting changes. They were close. Another few days and the oysters wouldn't become living ghosts, another name relegated to the endangered species lists.

"That's not going to help," Laura said.

"You could always stay with me," Ray replied, looking back toward his own home. "The girls would love that."

If she said yes, she knew she'd never finish the translation.

"I'm fine here. For now anyway. Who knows what the future holds? For now, if we fix the windows, that should be enough. The pattern's worked so far. I just need another week, tops, another week—"

"Another week for what? You want to tell me what's going on?"

Laura bit her lip. "It's nothing. Just another day or so and I'm done with Dad's old translation, that travelog from the Greek monk I told you about. It's mostly recountings of wildlife, lots of utopic scenery and descriptions of tropical fruit."

Ray nodded uncertainly, as if her words had slipped past him too fast to be believed.

"And what does that have to do with your little night visitors?"

Laura froze. "They must love poetry. It's in high demand."She tried to laugh off the comment, but the forced mirth died in the air between them.

"I see," Ray replied, eyes drifting back toward his house where the girls were playing basketball in the side yard. He began backing away, moving toward the road. He didn't offer to hold the plywood like usual, leaving Laura to use her knee and shoulders. She thought about calling after him, explaining everything, but she didn't want Ray to become a greater deterrent, one of those halting forces, a potential casualty.

But she also didn't want to drive him away, swept out of her life by a torrent of unhinged speculation.

Ray paused before he crossed the street.

"Are you still planning on joining us for dinner tonight?" he called to her. "We're doing lasagna."

"If I can get enough work done," Laura said, a spark of hope floating in her chest. Maybe everything really could be healed, happy endings not solely relegated to fiction.

"Door will be open. Just come over around six if you can. The girls will miss you if you skip out."

***

Laura had found her father, weeks after the diagnosis, crying before the aquarium in his living room, a holdover from lab days. The bottom was cluttered with mollusks: oysters and clams, mussels adhered to pieces of driftwood in the corner. Streams of green kelp drifted in the artificial current. The buzz of the filter burbled over his sobs.

His forehead was pressed against the glass when Laura pulled up a chair.

"We're definitely not going to make it to Greece," he said.

"We can still go. There's plenty of—"

"Not if I'm going to finish the poem."

"I thought you weren't sure whether that was the right move?"

"I need to leave something behind. Something that will help, otherwise it's all been a waste."

Laura's hand moved to her father's shoulders, rubbing circles into the fabric of his shirt.

"You did plenty of good, Dad. Think of the bay cleanup. Or the dovekie rehab. Or the plover monitoring sites. There's quite a list."

"But it's not enough," he replied.

"Is there ever enough?" she asked.

"I'd hope so."

They remained seated in the dim light of his living room, listening to the burble of the fish tank, observing the subtle movements of the mollusks, her father's entire life's work condensed to a single fifty-gallon tank and a stack of pages.

***

Laura hadn't left the lights on, certainly hadn't left the door unlocked, not with the completed manuscript on the desk, those final lines ready for recitation. But the cottage was wide open, light bleeding through the skylight and the singular window whose boards had been partially sheared away in the night, the things having left before shattering glass, only tearing the screen to tatters.

It was the closest they'd come to getting in.

Laura had a half-dozen donuts clutched in one hand, a bottle of hand-pressed grapefruit juice in the other. She figured she deserved a treat before the end...or the beginning, whatever came after her reading by the water.

The manuscript was exact in its instruction:

These words must be spoken in sight of the sea,

over waves,

carried on tides,

washing low to all ears.

Did oysters have ears? she'd wondered as she wrote, a skip of joy in her throat. That joy deflated as she hesitantly opened the cottage door, holding the donuts before her like a shaking, gluten-heavy shield. She wished she had the gun, or the hammer, or the knife, anything beyond a box of cheap baked goods.

Ray sat on the couch, manuscript pages stacked neatly beside him, the last left in his hand as his eyes traced the remaining words.

"How'd you get in?" she asked, putting down the donuts on her small dining table.

He raised a keyring from his lap without looking up from the page. "You gave me the spares when I installed the locks, remember?"

"That tracks, but why are you here? It's not like the pages call to you like they call to them," she replied.

Ray lifted a small shoulder bag with a patch depicting a goat-headed god and the name of a metal band sewn to the fabric. "You left this last night."

Laura hadn't been able to resist the lasagna.

"Can you just put those down? I worked really hard on them and I can totally explain what they all mean and..."

"I don't know if there's much to explain. The text is pretty straight forward on our options," Ray said, finally looking up, eyes red as if he'd been crying moments ago. "Are you actually going to read this? Have you thought about what it might mean for my girls if it's real? What it means for you and me?"

"If I don't read that, your daughters are going to be murdering neighbors for a bottle of water. Do you really want to be looking over your shoulder the rest of your life waiting for someone to do the same to them? There's no more ping-pong in the apocalypse. No sleepovers. No love. That's what's ahead."

"You don't know that," Ray replied, hand slowly moving through his beard. Over her shoulder, the sun had begun to set, the shortest day of the year only a week away. Winter's chill rushed through the open door, the lap of the sea failing to soothe the tension.

"Some people don't believe science, but I'm not one of them. Neither was my father," Laura said.

"There's always hope...always other options. Your father was real big on hope."

"This was the last thing he wanted." Laura didn't know how true that was, but the words came with confidence. She had to do this for him, after that night by the fish tank.

Before Ray could reply, the sound of something sloshing out of the water crept through the open door, wet and bulky, shifting its weight through the sand. Laura swore, rushing back to the door and slamming it shut, turning the twin deadbolts in place. Ray and Laura held each other's gaze from across the room before their eyes drifted to the unboarded window. A shadowed figure stood there, dripping seaweed from its massive frame. Laura didn't really know what she was looking at. The thing's body was amorphous and many limbed, barnacle-crusted, its head too high to view through the small opening.

"Not tigers," Ray said, eyes wide.

"Not tigers," Laura replied.

"Do you still have that gun?"

"What? Like I'd throw it in the ocean or something with this thing hanging around?" she said, hurrying to the small table beside her bed, unearthing the revolver from within.

"So, I'm going to shoot it and we're going to run back and get the girls. We'll get out of here and go read that poem. That will fix things, right?" Ray asked, gesturing for Laura to give him the gun.

"You want to read it together?" she asked, brain snagging on the implications as she handed over the weapon.

"Sure, I wouldn't let you do it alone. I..."

The sounds of something else sliding across the deck cut him off. There were a second and third body moving over the boards, others dragging their skin over the cement seawall, pressing through beach sand as they scaled the incline. From the noise, it was hard to pinpoint an exact number. It was safe to say many, all drawn to the final iteration of the poem, far more than the eight bullets in the revolver could handle.

"What do we do?" Ray asked, eyes traveling from one boarded window to the next.

"We wait. This happens every night. When the sun comes up, they usually just go away. They're kind of dumb, if I'm being honest."

"But what if they're not dumb this time? What if they get in?" Ray said, pointing to the only unobscured pane of glass, the seaweed-wrapped creature outside pawing at the portal.

"Then we go back to your first plan and hope they can't run fast," Laura replied, retrieving the knife she'd stashed behind the television.

Ray nodded, moving to stand next to Laura before the window. The last gasps of sunlight sank into the sea, casting a final orange blear across the creature's waterlogged skin. Then the evening's shadows were all consuming, everything through the slim portal fading to grayscale. Laura could smell the sweat wicking off Ray, could hear his heartbeat pulse in her ear. She was glad she wasn't alone on her last night in the cabin. She was glad at least one of her questions had been answered.

Together.

Not separate.

Now, all that was left was to find out what the poem would do to their world. If the words would tear some rent in the ocean floor and suck down all the sludge and smog, the pollutants and plastics and chemicals that never should have been...or would it vomit up more and more of the blind creatures who stalked about her home, scraping at the boards, hungry for what hid within?

Laura tightened her grip on the knife, leaning into Ray's side as they waited for morning to come.

***

It took three hours for the creatures to pull down the boards, leaving only bare glass between Laura and Ray and the gathered horde outside. The light from within made it hard to see much beyond their own reflections. Fangs bled through, and seaweed-wrapped limbs, but there were so many bodies pressing against the cabin's walls, it was impossible to separate one silhouette from the next or see the ocean beyond. The single bullet and run plan was looking grimmer with each passing moment as the cabin's frame quaked under pressure. Then a window cracked in the eastern wall, a spider web of fractals creeping through the glass.

"I'm saying the skylight's our only way out," Laura said, pointing to the ceiling and the water stains ringing the aperture. "We've got to push the couch over."

"I thought you said waiting was the best option," Ray said, nervously chewing his lip, eyes darting from one exposed window to the next.

"I don't think there've ever been this many. We need to improvise or we're screwed," she said, bending to wrap an arm around the old sofa, pushing it across the hardwood. Ray bent to help as they aligned the furniture with the lowest point of the skylight. The ceilings weren't high, but they needed an added step if they were going to get out.

Laura stood on the back of the couch, Ray steadying her thigh with his free hand. She twisted the knob, opening the skylight to the chill night air. The mechanism was old and rusted and fought her at every turn as her home continued to shiver under the press of the creatures' mass. Eventually the skylight opened wide enough for their bodies to slip through, once Laura pushed the screen out of the way.

"When I'm out, hand me the pages," she said, pulling herself up.

Ray did as he was asked, pushing the gathered poem through the skylight once Laura steadied herself on the roof. Then he followed, revolver tucked into the waistband of his pants, metal cylinders clinking against one another, reminding them of the eight bullets, the eight chances they had to clear a path through the swarm.

"Swarm" was the only way to describe the gathering. Laura looked out over the sea of huddled bodies stretching down the beach as more and more emerged from the ocean. She looked over her shoulder to see if they were approaching Ray's house down the road, but most seemed to orbit her small cabin, never wandering far from her sun-like pull.

"There's no way...no way we're making it to the girls," Ray said.

"There's one way. Maybe. I'm still not sure, but I don't think we have another option," Laura said, sifting through the pages as she climbed to the cabin's peak, the moon's glow barely enough to make out the words written there. "We're close enough to the water and I can clearly see the ocean. The tide can carry these words to whatever ears it wants to."

Below, the creatures continued to dismantle the cabin, pulling shingles from the walls, dragging nails from boards, shattering glass. Laura didn't know how much longer the building could remain upright, how long before it pitched over and tossed them into the throng of grasping limbs and gnashing teeth.

"How long will it take you to read it?" Ray asked, hurriedly flipping on the light of his smartphone, aiming the beam over her shoulder so she could see.

"I don't think that matters anymore. This is either going to work or it isn't."

"Can't you just tell me it will? I need something to go on. Something—" Ray said, words seizing in his throat. His eyes turned to his home and the dim glow filtering through his front windows, his girls somewhere within, possibly unaware of what their father was facing, possibly hiding in fear of what lurked beyond their front porch. Laura didn't want the last thought she left Ray with to be one of despair, so she lied.

"Oh, it's totally going to work. A hundred percent. No doubt in my mind. Just hold that light steady and we'll be fine."

As Laura began to read, the creatures gathered below stopped pushing against the cabin, stepping back, tilting their heads toward the sound of her voice. It was as if the words were familiar, as if they were waiting for what came next. Laura didn't know what the final canto would bring, but their stasis gave her hope. The cabin wouldn't collapse after all. Maybe there was still a chance to be the healer her father sought. Maybe the oysters and the fish and the gulls and everyone else weren't doomed.

Laura flipped to the next page, the words unspooling from her tongue as if they'd always been waiting there, waiting for the right moment to slip free.

FENCES AND FULL MOONS

They'd accepted that Cam was a werewolf. Invested in the thick steel chains, silver jewelry, and poured cement kennel. His father, Clark, watched fifty-seven YouTube videos from other parents discussing building techniques, how to sink footings deep, wrap fencing beneath the structure, wire a solar array on the kennel's roof to generate electricity. He wanted his son to have the best of the best, despite the back aches and the scars on his knuckles. He'd never been handy before the symptoms manifested.

The kennel had done its job for fifteen cycles before Cam got out and ate the chickens. It was a small flock, only enough to supply their family with eggs for breakfast, nothing for the farmstand Clark and his wife, Val, dreamed of adding to the front lawn.

Cam finally pried apart the gate, tore through the padlocks, and ignored the jolt from the electrified fence.

"Maybe a moat would have been better," Clark said, welding the gate back in place.

"But what if I drown?" Cam asked at his elbow.

Cam was in fourth grade, hair sheared into a bowl cut, front teeth coming in crowded. He was short for his age, a fact his classmates never failed to mention at recess. Clark joked about them saying that to him on a full moon, but Val said he needed to stop talking like that. He wasn't trying to encourage violence, only to let Cam know he wasn't helpless.

"Did you ever see a dog that couldn't swim?" Clark asked, swinging the patchwork door into place, rattling the locks.

"No," Cam replied.

"Then I think a werewolf would be fine."

"So, I'd swim across?"

"Yeah, I...guess that defeats the purpose."

"Sorry, Dad," Cam said, toying with the butterfly net his mother gave him that morning, trying to get the boy's mind off the feathers stuck in his teeth. He loved insects: beetles, grasshoppers, butterflies. Moths and stick bugs distracted him from the crimson smears Val washed out of the grass, all that blood pooled in the kennel.

"More locks it is," Clark said, satisfied with his handiwork. "You remember anything from last night?"

"Not much," Cam replied.

"What do you remember?" Clark asked, walking into the enclosure, sidestepping the water trough fed from a rain barrel. He prodded the stained mattress with his foot, leaned close to sniff for mold. The waterproof pillow-top was a steep buy. They'd put it on the credit card, despite ridiculous interest rates. Clark could go without take-out lunches during his post office shifts for the next few months for the sake of Cam's sleep habits.

"Nothing..." Cam said, not meeting his father's eye.

Clark knew his son's memory didn't shut off when the moon was full, but he wouldn't push him on the matter. They had enough to deal with without adding another layer to the equation. Two more nights of transitions lay ahead.

**

The locks held the first night.

Then, the shearing of metal on metal swept Clark from dreams. Through their second-story window, he saw Cam, teeth bared, snout nosing through the welded patch on the kennel door, metal bent out of shape. One paw passed through, then the other, tearing at the ground on the other side, fighting to drag his narrow hips through the opening.

Clark descended the steps two at a time, pulling his flannel jacket on as he pushed open the screen door. The night was chill, the feel of rain in the air, grass slick with dew. He nearly lost his footing as he lunged for his son, Cam slipping from the kennel, bounding toward the tree line on the far side of the yard.

"You need to calm down," Clark whispered into his son's pointed ear, arms locked around his body as Cam's jaws snapped about his face, wet and sharp, never finding purchase.

As the two struggled in the grass, claws dragging blood from exposed skin, Clark could see the years stretching away from them. He'd read about teenage werewolves. The added strength, the lust, the taste for larger, more intelligent prey. Every month, the struggle would get worse. They'd need thicker fencing, higher voltage wire, ropes and chains that would never be easy to secure.

Clark could only use his own arms as restraints for so long.

That would be his reality, month after month.

The tree line wasn't far off. Acres of dense deciduous forest ran for miles. Clark could ease his hold, let Cam sprint for the woods. They were vast enough to swallow anything, to never spit it back out. It would be easy. A release, a push, a reset. Val would never know it was intentional.

He loosened his grip, but tightened it before Cam could gain purchase.

That wasn't what Clark wanted.

He twisted onto his back, arm clamping Cam's jaws in an improvised headlock. Cam whimpered, hot breath drifting from his nostrils. Clark wasn't going to abandon his child to the wilderness, to the wild voices swelling in his throat.

There were training techniques he'd read about, methods of containment, werewolf mindfulness, a way to press rage down inside Cam so he could actually use the mattress they'd spent all that money on, instead of dragging bleeding livestock beneath the roof beams.

Clark heaved, lifting Cam's sprawling body into the kennel. He couldn't repatch the fence, not that night. Instead, Clark carried Cam to the bed, sitting, leaning back against the fencing. Lupine muscles slowly eased into Clark's embrace, fight fleeing.

The sun would rise in several hours.

Clark could wait until then, until his son morphed back into the pale boy with the bowl cut, the boy whose hunger was no longer insatiable.

THE TAP, TAP, TAP OF A BEAK

1.

When the train rattled, the bones in the mahogany box at Alva's side rattled back. It sounded as if the two were in conversation, parsing out where each was headed. The *thwock* and *click* of calcium matched the grind of rusted rails beneath them, slow and predictable. Alva thought she could follow their thread, the nervousness and anxiety, but the language was lost beyond general emotion.

The station was still three hours away and the dinner cart was about to open its doors.

There wasn't enough time to decipher an entire dialect.

***

When the train first departed, a man and a woman sat across from Alva on the green upholstered benches. After the first half-hour, they expressed their discomfort with the incessant noise of bones.

"I'm sure they aren't talking about you," Alva said to the couple.

"That's not it," the man said, eyes moving to the box.

"I just can't read with noise around me," the woman added.

"Then train travel might not be your best option," Alva said as the two exited into the hall to find another compartment.

***

Alva had spent the past fifteen years with the bird—or the bird's parents, or their parents—studying avian patterns and characteristics, their dwindling habitat, mating songs, and dietary restrictions. Larry, as she affectionately named the last known individual Gabri's tufted woodpecker, hadn't been able to find a mate, no nest cavity large enough to hold his future offspring, even if there were viable females within range.

The forest had thinned. Trees no longer reached necessary heights.

Alva gathered Larry's body from the base of a rotting cedar, the same cedar she visited every day at exactly 5:30 a.m. to check on her subject. She held his body, searching for breath, a subtle tremor through feather and wing, but he was still, and the species' genetic line had come to an end.

It took less than a month for muscle and ligament to melt from the bird's hollow bones. Alva constructed a rot cage on her deck to keep neighborhood cats at bay. She plucked the feathers to add to the archives at her university, but the skeleton belonged to The Heap. They had enough taxidermied subjects. One more wouldn't make any difference.

Skin decayed. Varied shades of decomposition unfolded before her. The smell was only intolerable the first week while the carrion beetles did their work. She kept her windows closed through the August heat. When the skeleton lay bleached, she gathered Larry and installed him in the mahogany box her father made.

There's only so much time, he'd said.

The beak was the only recognizable part of the bird she'd once known, three inches long, deep blue, one shade south of navy.

Alva opened the box to see if the beak was in motion, squawking through syllables unknown during life. All she found was the tiny shoulder blades and leg bones rolling about, beak tucked in the corner. The skull was on its side, one empty eye socket gazing toward the dull overhead lights, looking for familiar trees.

2.

Alva's parents brought her to The Heap when she was too young to understand the implications of the vast landscape of bone. Thousands of species had been deposited on the site, femurs and skulls crowding together, piled under the sky, a bleached mountainside. Ribcages arched out of the slurry like thousands of rounded, unmarked graves. Alva's mother led her through the spruce and pine forest to get to the edge where leaf litter gave way to sand, sediment half-composed from eroded calcium. Alva remembered it like a beach, with a crashing wave rising above her, paler than the moon.

"Why do they do this?" Alva said, turning to her father who trained a camera on her.

"It's a reminder," he said. "Of what's been lost. Of our role in things."

The red *Record* light flickered like candle flame before her face.

Alva hated how he was always recording. Her parents were part of a nature documentary team, chronicling the rise and fall of certain species; the wolves gone missing from Maine, the elusive nests of bald eagles. Their television show aired at 6 a.m. each Saturday before cartoons bounced across screens. Education was for early-risers. Mischief and mayhem for all the rest. The episode they were filming was focused on The Heap, trying to identify the skeletons of animals they had once met in real life. The producer wanted them to find the Mexican grizzly bear or the Caspian tiger, but her father said they couldn't promise anything. There were many bones, many skulls similar enough to confuse one species from the next.

"I'll find the tiger," Alva said when they reached the bone-thick shore, hesitating before stepping onto The Heap.

Her mother gasped and pulled her back.

"Oh no no. We don't touch the bones. That's disrespectful. We can look from a distance, use the camera to gather detail, but we have to do it from back here," she said, straightening Alva's hair.

"You don't want their ghosts following you home, do you?" her father said, winking from behind the camera.

"They don't do that... Right?" Alva said, her complexion dimming.

"You never know," her mother said. "There's more than one reason for The Heap. You can't be too careful with the dead."

"They're almost as bad as the living," her father said with a laugh, unfolding his tripod and securing his camera on the mounting plate. He waved the sound guy to his side, gesturing to where they would film, framing the shot with his hands as Alva's mother straightened her own hair, squinting at the bones. The skulls of primates and reptiles gazed back, a thousand hollow eyes sunken into the mountainside.

Alva tried to count them, but lost track before her father started filming.

"In no other place can you find thousands of years of life laid bare, an open grave to centuries past. Join us today as we search for our long-lost friends..." her mother continued as the camera panned away, its lens gathering up the landscape of clavicles, femurs, and mandibles stretching to the horizon.

3.

The door to Alva's compartment slid open, coasting on oiled rollers before clattering to a halt. A man in a dark suit with a large Adam's apple leaned in from the harsh light beyond. Alva had just returned from the dining cart, where grilled cheese and tomato soup had been the only vegetarian option on the menu. The warm broth sloshed in her stomach as she startled from the draft of her latest article on Gabris' mating routines cradled in her lap.

"They said I'd find you here." The man seated himself across from Alva without invitation.

"Who said what?" Alva's hand moved to the box, her fingers wrapping around the edge.

"This couple in the dining cart. They said I'd find a bone-bearer down here."

Alva didn't consider herself a bone-bearer by contemporary standards. It was a term often used for people who were little more than armchair archeologists, those who uncovered bones on family vacations or in their yards, but never properly identified them. It had become a trend. Individuals who unearthed the bones of someone's house cat buried in the rose bushes and turned it into an excuse to take photos for social media at The Heap. Alva was a scientist. She knew the woodpecker at her side was the last of its kind. The bird needed to be added to the collection, for posterity, for its soul to rest. And if she was completely honest with herself, her parents' talk of ghosts had stuck with her. Alva didn't want Larry haunting her for the rest of her life, looming over her sushi dates and medical appointments, scowling over mistyped field notes.

"Can I see it?" he said, pointing at the box.

"I'd prefer not to open it here," Alva said. "The bones might get tossed around."

"You've probably got some squirrel with a birth defect. Or one of those two-headed snakes. People never have a final specimen these days."

"No, this is definitely the last Gabri's tufted woodpecker. I spent enough time with him to know."

The man cocked an eyebrow. "You're a biologist?"

"An ornithologist. Lar—this bird was the focus of my study, my career, his whole flock anyway."

The man's face sprinted through a number of emotions, settling on inquisitive awe. He went silent, staring at the box, listening to the hollow rattle within. Alva could see his mental gymnastics, scanning memories for the bird, any familiarity he might have. People often did so when she explained her work, only for Alva to swear there was little chance they'd ever seen one unless they spent a lot of time in a very specific swamp in Georgia, miles away from civilization.

"How much will you sell him for?" the man said.

"What?"

"I buy skeletons. It's a hobby. Kind of like taxidermy, only with less fur and skin," the man said. "Smells better."

"Are you kidding?"

"Nope. I do this all the time. You catch people heading out to The Heap with all sorts of oddities. There's only so many trains heading north."

"And scientists actually sell you their bones?"

"Nine times out of ten. I know how strapped you guys are. The whole funding issue. But it's not like I do anything weird with the bones. I arrange them, put them on display, all the good stuff. None of that necro—"

"So you run a museum?" Alva cut in, not wanting the conversation to veer any further down dark paths.

"Nope again. Private collection. I don't want random people in my house. They make things dirty."

Alva shook her head. If Larry wasn't going to end up on The Heap, he would be preserved in the museum at her university or that of another institution. Larry was like a child to her. She'd watch each stage of his growth: first flight, early meals, the original hole he bore into a dead pine. She could never give him to a man who'd use Larry as a mantle decoration. The thought churned her stomach.

"I appreciate your concern for my underpaid colleagues, but I'm going to pass. If you wouldn't mind leaving, that would be great." Alva returned to her article.

"Fifty-thousand dollars. Are you really passing that up? I'm sure you've got rent to pay, credit card bills piling up," the man said.

Holy hell, that is a lot of money, Alva thought. She wasn't behind on rent, but her bank account was regularly barren. She'd practically given up on the idea of savings.

"I'm all set," she said.

The man sighed, straightening the front of his pants as he stood. "Suit yourself. Still another two hours until we arrive at the station. When you change your mind, I'm in compartment eighty-one."

"Enjoy the rest of your trip," Alva said without looking up.

The man stepped out and closed the door. The bones at her side seemed to chide and cackle even louder than before. *Must be old tracks*, Alva told herself, underlining a poorly articulated sentence.

4.

Larry lived in the upper limbs of a deceased red cedar, his home a fist-sized hole in the trunk. Alva sat a few feet out from the base, reclining in a canvas chair, binoculars pressed to her eyes. She had a notebook in hand, enough food and water to get to sunset. She pulled a tape recorder from the bag at her feet. The month of May was the start of mating season. No one else had captured the song of the Gabri's tufted woodpecker, not well anyway. There was very little chance of the song becoming a duet, but stranger things had happened.

The dark blue beak emerged from the hole, followed by the rest of Larry's white and black feathers, his orange eyes huge like a cartoon, comical in their odd sadness. They reminded Alva of the characters on the children's shows she watched, those few she'd seen on her rare stretches between her parents' assignments. They'd never spent much time in one place, addling through homeschool in the back of busses and airplanes. Math had never been easy.

Alva had pen pals, a friend here and there from brief stints in varied apartments, but no one she really considered close. Besides her mother and father and the odd classmate in her long-ago graduate program, she'd probably spent more time with Larry than anyone else.

Isolation usually didn't weigh on her, but lately, with the lack of returned mating calls, she was beginning to dwell on missed connections, a fairly peopleless past. When she began her study fifteen years ago, she thought she would be the one to save the woodpeckers, bring them back from the brink with well executed land conservation proposals and tracking plans. But the Gabri's were only one of a thousand birds on the endangered list, and the public's attention turned more toward bright plumage than obscene eyes.

She made progress, but never in the right direction. On a number of fronts.

Alva leaned back in her canvas chair, quickly sketching the bird on the edge of his perch, neck inclined to the sky, high notes trilling from his throat. Larry paused after reciting several refrains. Alva could almost see him tilting his head toward the distant forest, listening, pleading with the empty air to return his call. After a moment, he thudded his beak against the tree's trunk, rolling through the second phase of his song, the hollow *ratatat* swelling with repetition.

Clouds passed. The twitter of a warbler drifted from a copse of pine, but no other woodpecker replied.

***

The performance went on for the better part of the morning, Larry repeating the process, only to be let down by the result.

Alva knew how it felt to be ignored, left behind by the world. All her published papers seemed to go unread. Her proposals at town and state meetings met with drooping eyes and the occasional yawn. Her parents were kind people, but obsessive, wrapped up in their own work. She never liked to call their absence childhood neglect, despite what her therapist said.

Beyond that, she also knew the chances of another Gabri's living nearby were unlikely.

Alva cupped a hand to her mouth and imitated the call, producing a shaky rendition of Larry's vocalization.

The bird perked up at the noise, head tilting toward her call. He seemed to wait for a reiteration, confirmation that his senses weren't lying. Alva couldn't imitate the sound again, couldn't show him where the noise was coming from. The action would ruin her study, and could discourage the bird.

Without a second refrain, Larry lurched off the branch before two awkward flaps carried him between neighboring trees on the hunt for the source of the call. Alva traced his path around pines with her binoculars, unsure whether she was being cruel, whether false hope sped decline. She prayed her call would have the opposite effect, but she packed up her gear anyway, not wanting to be present for Larry's return, to see what emotions flit across his large orange eyes.

5.

The money was a lot, Alva couldn't question that. She thought of all the expenses the sum would cover. The new mattress her lower back begged for. The night guard her dentist had been trying to persuade her to purchase for five years. *You carry the stress in your jaw*, he always said. So much menial suffering could be cured with a simple exchange, but that didn't stop Alva from slinking by the man's cabin as the train pulled into the station, the hiss of air brakes breathing into the night air. A shadow flickered across the compartment's glass door, but she was gone, hurrying for the exit, pulling her rolling luggage at her heels, the mahogany box tucked under her arm.

From the platform, she descended the stairs, breathing hard, the smell of her own sweat sour with each hastened step. She hadn't been in running shape since letting her gym membership lapse two years ago, but she couldn't allow the man to catch up. If the offer was raised, she couldn't predict what she would do.

That money would make whatever came next in life an easier transition.

Alva shrugged off the thought.

The street leading from the station was poorly lit. Several storefronts displayed tourist attire backlit by low bulbs. T-shirts and hoodies showed depictions of The Heap, some with cartoonish smiling bones for the kids, others with postcard-like vistas for the rest. Each proclaimed the wearer's visit to The Heap, that *I played my part*. Alva nearly spat on the glass as she hurried to her hotel.

The idea of playing their part, she thought, only came to most people once there was none left to play. They could save the living rather than honor the dead. They could save so much sorrow, and such a long train ride.

Over her shoulder, down the narrow street, a man's figure stepped from beneath the station's awning. Alva wasn't sure if the silhouette belonged to her man, or just any man. Either way, she ducked into the hotel lobby, nearly knocking into the bellhop, a slew of apologies on her lips.

If the man from the train knew she wouldn't take the money, Alva didn't know what else he might offer.

6.

"I have your mother and your mother has me," her father said, leaning back in a rocking chair on their front porch. His beard had gone white, his knuckles crooked with arthritis.

"And?" Alva asked, knowing where her father's insinuations led.

They'd taken to spending nights on the front porch of her parents' retirement house, a renovated cabin on sixteen acres of fallow farmland. They watched swallows pick apart swarms of gnats and mosquitos over the old pastures. Alva could only make the trip every few months. She feared time away from the forest.

"You've always got to think what happens after," her father said.

She became defensive. "There might not be an after. Things could change. It's not like every woodpecker is tagged. Look at that guy with the extinct foxes under his shed. There could always be another flock up the river, or by the mountains, or..."

"We've seen how this usually goes," her mother said, placing a sweating bottle of beer in her daughter's hand, then taking the seat next to her husband. "You know why we rarely did follow-up shows, right?"

Alva nodded. "Kids TV is supposed to be less depressing than reality."

"That's one way to put it," her mother said. "But we're getting a bit off topic. Are you still trying those dating sites?"

Alva sighed. "Can we not talk about this? Please?"

"You're telling me there's no attractive professors at the college?" her father asked. "No interesting new speakers at one of your conferences?"

"Things are quiet both in the real world and on the digital front," Alva said, sipping her beer. "I've been practicing my mating call though." Then she produced a comical series of tweets and rapped her knuckle on the side of the house. "I hope you brought your binoculars. They're going to come tearing across the field any moment."

Both her parents laughed.

They moved away from the topic. No one wanted to sprint down dark roads any longer. The conversation drifted between her recent scholarly paper and her mother's latest photography project, documenting the decline of abandoned barns across the countryside. She was talking about making a book, about how she preferred to see man-made structures slump into the earth rather than watch forests and other ecosystems disappear.

The sun set as the swallows moved back to their roosts, the beat of wings diminishing as stars sparked overhead.

"I made something for you," her father said as her mother took their accumulated empties to the kitchen.

Her father lifted a wooden box from beneath his seat and passed it to Alva. She turned the box over in her hands, inspecting the hinges, the smoothed mahogany, the odd coffin-like construction. On the days he wasn't at the recording studio narrating low budget documentaries on shellfish, he had begun making bird houses. There was no entrance hole, no mount for the box's back.

"If you ever need it," he said, pausing. "I seriously hope you don't, but just in case, you don't want to be without."

"Thanks, Dad," she replied, tucking it under her feet, unable to look at it for more than a second, envisioning her entire life's work reduced to the narrow confines within.

7.

Clutching the box to her chest, bones rattling, Alva left the hotel as the sun crept over distant hills. She followed side streets out of town to where nature paths cut through surrounding forests. She had brought a map but did not consult it, instead recalling routes her parents had taken during visits years ago. Alva tried to focus on the path, but she glanced behind for shadows, listened for footsteps. She had to be quick.

The path entered the forest, an avenue of pine needles and dirt worn smooth from years of traffic. The forest sung around her: birds and insects, squirrels crossing tree branches, frogs hiccuping near vernal pools. The trees created a corridor, branches woven together, glimpses of the sky's bright cathedral above.

At the path's end, the shadow of the woods dropped off to stark, nearly blinding white. The sun embellished the huge accumulation of pale bones, washing over the dusty shoreline that circled The Heap. The mountain was vast, steeper than she remembered. Millions of dissected skeletons blotted out the forest behind its peak. All the color bled from her vision until The Heap met the sky. The day was already hot and growing warmer in the open clearing. Skulls gathered her attention, empty eyes and gaping mouths strewn between femurs and spines. Alva fought childhood inclinations to count them, to name them, to construct lives for those already gone.

A number of gray-back gulls circled overhead. Occasionally they would land and peck about the great mound, searching for sinew and muscle, something not yet rotted. Alva couldn't shoo them off without climbing over the bones, and that wasn't going to happen. Like her father said, she didn't want ghosts following her home.

***

Alva walked the boundary between forest and The Heap, free hand running along the box's lid, listening to the bones rattle inside, jarred with each step.

"So this is afterward," she said to herself, sitting down, reclining against an oak.

She undid the latch. Larry's skull peered back at her, empty eyes gathering a last look before they were separated. She willed the beak to quiver and speak, to tell her she hadn't wasted her time, that someone else would read her research and not make the same mistakes. Alva's singular purpose in life was now relegated to the past, her days rearranging themselves into uncertain futures. She needed the bird's blessing. Even a single kind squawk would do.

He'd been so chatty on the train, why not now?

There was a stillness, then the beak jostled, blue tip prodding the box's side. The rest of the bones swirled about, driftwood caught in a strong sea-bound current. Startled, Alva almost dropped the miniature coffin. The coo and chortle of the bird's call rattled through a nonexistent throat, whistling out between parted beak.

She'd thought the couple on the train had been exaggerating.

Alva rose to her feet.

As soon as she stood, her legs were swept from beneath her. A booted heel met her shoulder and sent her sprawling. Larry's coffin tumbled away. The man from the train towered above her, smiling, suit damp about the collar, dirt smeared around the cuffs.

"That was a lot of money you passed up," he said, pulling a knife from inside his suit.

Alva lunged at the box, but the man stepped between, heel crushing her hand into the dry earth. There was the crack of bone. Sharp pain coursed up her arm like a flood of broken glass. Alva pulled her hand in and curled herself tight, two fingers bent out of alignment.

"This is the other reason they always take the money, all your scientist buddies," the man said, bending to scoop up the box. "I was going to get the bird one way or another. You knew that."

"But why—why do you need him? You have so many already," Alva gasped through clenched lips.

"If this is the last, then I must have it." He regarded the box. "Have you ever possessed something no one else has? It's exhilarating! Close to magic. I've worked very very hard to build my collection. You wouldn't believe the number of hours it takes to get these things right."

"But he needs to be in The Heap with the others. He won't be able to—"

"Nope. Old wives' tales. I've taken so many of these and you don't see a single ghost harassing me. I sleep great! No nightmares."

The man was practically vibrating, his skin flush. His hands tremored as he lifted the lid.

Alva could rush him, she could drive her shoulder through his bulk... But no, the pain in her hand wouldn't let her.

The man in the dark suit sucked a breath through his teeth. Then he grew still, head tilted, staring into the mahogany casket. "What?" he asked no one.

The whistle of the woodpecker's call sounded again from within, followed by the scuttle of bone against wood.

The man dropped the box. It landed open in the sand. The bird's skeleton stepped from the confines, talons grasping hinges, beak prodding the air as if scenting direction. He took a single step on unsure feet, before testing his wings, finding lift, rising from his perch. Bone creaked against bone. He hovered for a moment, a vision of death treading air, before alighting on Alva's shoulder.

"Less work for me. Already assembled," the man said, eyes wide as he retrieved the box. "Just get in, little guy, and I won't break any more of your mom's fingers."

Larry sang again, repeating his mating call, fast and clean.

The man stepped forward, shadow falling over Alva's prone form, knife in hand.

Alva withdrew, inching backward, from him and the clattering noise. The sound was low at first, but built as skulls and spines pulled together, ribs leading to hips leading to legs, hooves and talons falling into place, rising in cacophony. A gale of sand and bone dust rose around the assembly, clouding The Heap in a harsh haze.

The man in the dark suit finally turned as hundreds of species stepped from the swirling sediment: ancient elk and wolves, large cats, eagles and lizards. Something akin to a dinosaur loomed over the gathering, jaw draped open, teeth the size of butcher's knives. They approached in a horde, eyeless sockets trained on the man, metatarsals and phalanges pushing through sand.

The man glanced from the gathering to the forest path, fidgeting with his knife which now seemed more comical than threatening. He took three steps before the creatures dropped on him in a cascading wave of bone, hooves and paws rushing over the ground, jaws wide. Their defined figures collapsed, sweeping him under. His screams were lost by the resonance of skeletons coming apart, separating again into their mismatched chaos.

The surge of bones washed up against Alva's feet as if she had been dangling her toes in the surf. The Heap had shifted several feet toward the woods. Alva searched for the punctuation of color among them, the dark suit, a splash of crimson blood, but she found nothing. Only the sea of white regaining calm, placid and unyielding.

Larry scuttled across Alva's shoulder, nipped her ear, and fluttered down to her feet, where he perched on the tip of her shoe. She reached for him. He tilted his skull at her, empty eyes meeting her own. Then he flew off, moving over the rise of The Heap, climbing higher to the summit before his bones separated, form becoming formless.

8.

Alva leaned against the trunk of an oak, cradling her broken hand, eyes fixed on the spot Larry had dropped from the sky. His casket lay at her feet. She considered burying it, saying a brief prayer before wandering home, but that was unnecessary. She'd seen the gathering, the ranks of the dead. That was enough of a send-off, pomp and pageantry fitting of the last Gabri's tufted woodpecker.

You've always got to think of what happens after, she heard her father say in the back of her head.

She still had her job, her meager salary that kept the lights on, her unsuccessful dating apps. There were other species that needed attention: night parrots and crested ibis, Egyptian vultures and California condors. Unfortunately, there would never be a shortage of names on the list. She could spend the weekend at her parents' house, following the swallows, contemplating the last paper she'd write about her time in the forest and what actually came after.

There had to be a final chapter, death and the wave of bones not solely restricted to memory. She didn't know who'd publish something like that, what academic journals would call the work anything other than fiction. She'd worry about that later. Even if her paper went ignored like all the others, at least the writing would exist, at least she had tried. Compassion would have to come from others.

Maybe the article would be a character study, a look at modern psyches and where they failed the human species and all those around them. Superfluous desires outweighed the need for healthy ecosystems, healthy relationships in general, a never-ending divorce from reality sprawling through decades.

Alva didn't know the paper's final form, but she knew where to start. The words twitched in the fingers of her non-broken hand, a ghost keyboard laid out before her, playing just beyond her reach.

The first sentence came to her as rough bark wore against her shoulder blades. *The number of men who prefer to horde bones rather than protect life is alarming.*

Without further hesitation, she returned to the forest path, leaving the coffin with the distributed remains.

She didn't want to miss the last train home.

Someone else would put the casket to better use.

THE BURNT FLOOR

Bronski and Janet saved for three years but could only afford a room on the burnt floor. The hotel was a fifteen-minute drive from the amusement park, all those lanky spotted mammals behind high fences, the wavelike rollercoasters plummeting from frozen peaks. The first two floors were four-star accommodations. The third, one point five.

The room contained two beds, frames scarred black. The ceiling was veined charcoal, the rugs blossoming with scorch marks, black ripples on a white pond. Only one wall retained its original green-and-white wallpaper. The rest curled, blackened, exposing pale sheetrock beneath.

At least the beds had clean sheets. They looked clean anyway—Bronski couldn't smell much of anything through the respirator. Each of the kids wore one, too, in a child's size. The clear plastic window obscured little Becky's face, dimming her eyes, swallowing her cheeks beneath twin filters. Jeremy's was too small; the rubber straps sank into his neck, reddening his pale skin.

When they first started planning this vacation, years ago, Bronski and Janet had smiled at each other over the freedom it would bring, the shrugging off of responsibilities and anxieties. But then Janet's hours were reduced and Bronski's company stopped handing out Christmas bonuses, and by the time they checked the online box for the burnt room, they were no longer smiling.

Jeremy attempted to view the park from their window, but the smoked haze of the pane was too clotted. There was a spot at the corner where a previous guest had tried to scrape away the singed layer with a razor blade. It was the only clear spot, a window within a window. Jeremy bent, removing his respirator, unburdening his irritated skin, pressing his bare cheek to the pane, squinting.

Bronski sprinted to his son's side, snapping the mask back in place. "What did we say?" he asked.

"Sorry, Dad," his son replied.

"You can take it off outside. In here, you've got to be safe."

Then Bronski lowered himself to the small clear pane, searching for the castles of plastic and synthetic stone, those birthday cake lights strung along turrets. But he could only see his own reflection, framed by that ring of black char.

***

On the first day, they rode the roller coasters. Afterward, little Becky attempted to pet the lanky spotted mammals, a smile painted on her face. Bronski kept raising her up over his head, helping her get those extra feet. A staff member in a safari hat and cargo shorts scolded them, threatened to have them kicked out, but their family knew something about evasion and bled back into the crowd, an estuary emptying into the open sea.

Jeremy said it was the best day of his life, even though he'd thrown up all over himself and Becky after round three of rollercoastering.

Becky agreed as she wrung out her dress over a fountain with a marble shrew at its center.

"At least it doesn't smell as bad as the room," Becky said after adjusting her sodden outfit.

"Did you take your mask off?" Janet asked, turning on their daughter.

They'd told the kids the same thing that was in the waiver they signed at the front desk: the rooms were only carcinogenic if the air wasn't filtered.

"I had to itch my nose," Becky said.

Bronski shook his head, careful to not unseat the animal ears his children forced him to buy. "Just don't do it again, alright?"

***

Upon returning, they crossed through the immaculately draped entranceway, thick crimson carpet beneath their feet, golden curtains obscuring unblemished windows, the waft of chlorine spilling over from the indoor swimming pool. They passed two golden sphinxes on their way to the stairwell.

The elevator only went to the second floor.

Before they could push open the heavy pneumatic door, a bellhop ran over and sprayed them down with perfumed rose water. The children coughed and wiped at their eyes. Bronski made sure to hold his breath. The hotel called the practice "scent therapy," as if it were for the good of those residing on the burnt floor rather than the rest of their guests and the world at large. An employee sprayed the concoction whenever their family entered or exited the building, like passing through a carwash.

Bronski held open the stairwell door with one hand, drying his lips with the other.

Janet doled out the respirators as they climbed.

***

In the early morning, Bronski woke to what he thought were bird songs, maybe those swamp crows he'd read about in the guidebook. After the haze of sleep receded, the noise more closely resembled the sound of his children giggling, the elastic twang of rubber snapping into place over bare flesh. Bronski sat up, turning to where his two children lay in bed. They were still, frozen beneath the sheets, masks possibly askew. It was dark, made all the darker by the burnt sky overhead. Bronski wondered if it was his fear driving an auditory hallucination, all those whispered jokes from his coworkers about fire-retardant swimwear. The kids were probably fine.

Nestling back into his pillow, Bronski had flashes of what their vacation could have been if there were only more hours in the day or an eighth day of the week on which to earn overtime. But his company no longer offered overtime, just regular time, and the burnt floor was all they'd ever be able to afford. He tried to push the whispers from his mind.

He rolled over and slung an arm around Janet, pulling her close, letting himself believe he'd done right.

***

The next day was more rollercoastering. Banks of screens showed the kids as they screamed down long drops, as they screamed at boogeymen who emerged from behind fiberglass crypts, as they screamed as their spacecraft fell from orbit. Like everyone else in the park, Janet and Bronski never purchased the photos, only snapping grainy duplicates with their cellphones. A souvenir was still a souvenir.

Bronski hoped that was the only thing they carried home with them. He started to worry when little Becky began to cough uncontrollably after exiting a Western-themed Hey-Hey sing-along cart ride. The cough went on and on, wet and dry at the same time. Harsh to the ear.

"Too much singing, honey?" Janet asked, stooping to Becky's level, pulling her close.

"They played all my favorite songs," Becky stammered between coughs, a ropey line of snot connecting their shirts in a spiderweb weave. "I couldn't help it."

"You sang beautifully, dear," Janet replied, catching Bronski's eye, her brows furrowed in concern.

Everyone said you had to take the kids to the park before they got too old, before the magic wouldn't be magic. The years weren't slowing. If he had put off the trip a few more months, he would have put it off a few more months after that, and so on and so forth until he found himself crying at songs from their childhood as he dropped little Becky off at college.

No, now was the only time, regardless of the money, regardless of the room, regardless of the rash that was spreading around the contours of his mask where the gasket pressed tight to his cheeks. The kids deserved their three days at the park and Bronski deserved those three days where he could be present in their lives, not some blur rushing out the door at five in the morning, only reappearing after dinner had been cleared from the table.

***

"It's a great deal, but not that great," the woman behind the front desk said, a fake smile stretching her cheeks. She toyed with a pen and sketchpad, doodling little caricatures of human faces.

"But I thought we had access to the pool?" Bronski said, hand on Jeremy's shirtless shoulder, his swim trunks laced tight around his stomach, towel in hand.

"If you selected the upgraded package, yes, the pool would be all yours, but your reservation says you chose our economy option."

"Can't you just let us in, just this once? No one will notice."

"Oh, people will definitely notice, but I can bump you up to full access for another fifty dollars a night. This covers the sanitation fees for our third-floor guests. Would that work?" the woman asked, her doodle beginning to resemble Bronski, his sleep-deprived baggy eyes, the desperate frown carving his face.

"But we're already paying—"

Bronski's reply was cut short by a series of sneezes from Jeremy followed by a chorus of coughs. His son covered his face with his towel, bending low toward the plush carpets. The fit wouldn't stop.

"You should probably get that looked at," the woman said. "Somewhere not right in front of my desk."

Bronski wanted to scream, to tear the notepad from her hands and scribble out the insult of himself etched there, replacing the drawing with his own rendition of the woman and what he thought about her subpar service, but he couldn't ignore Jeremy's distress. Without another word, he steered his son toward the stairwell, through the perfumed mist of rose water.

"We'll just get you into the shower, right, bud? A shower's basically the same thing as a swimming pool, yeah? Just as good, I promise."

***

The third day was less rollercoastering, more snapshots with park fixtures. Men and women dressed as fairytale characters. Ridiculous confectionary streets. Castles that seemed to blot out the sun. Janet wanted to get a shot of their children in front of each landmark.

"Just put your arms around each other," Janet said, waving the children together before a man-made waterfall, an animatronic orangutan eternally peeling bananas to their left.

"Haven't we taken enough pictures?" Jeremy asked, his sunburned cheeks glistening, a labored wheeze accompanying the question. The kids had been lethargic since breakfast.

"There will never be enough pictures," Janet muttered as she snapped the shot, quiet enough only Bronski could hear her.

"Can we go to the pirate ship again?" Becky asked.

"Yeah, let's do the pirate thing again," Jeremy added, before a skull-rattling sneeze escaped from his mouth and nose.

Unlike the day before, a stream of black mucus coated his shirtfront, snot mixed with coal dust and char, a river of oil dripping onto the downtown sidewalk. He raised his hands, touching his nose, inspecting the black webbing, eyes growing wider with each second. Then he was screaming, and little Becky was screaming, and Janet was screaming, and a man dressed like a pantless opossum was escorting them to a white-walled service station behind the so-called lollipop factory. A tiny rhino attendant appeared from inside, wiping at

Jeremy's face with a towel, mopping up the black mucus, smothering his screams until they faded to whimpers.

"Staying on the burnt floor?" the pantless opossum asked Bronski, pulling him aside as the rhino gave the children and Janet rainbow-colored lollipops the size of basketballs.

"How did you—"

"This happens all the time. We have a protocol now," the opossum said as he scratched his distended belly.

"But the manager said it was safe."

"Hey, I'm not casting judgement, but I need you and yours out of my clean-up room. We charge by the minute."

"Are you serious?"

"Don't worry, the lollipops are on the house. Just get going, alright?"

Bronski never imagined he'd be intimidated by a giant pantless opossum, but he also never imagined he'd put his family at risk for a few blurry photos on a water slide and a shot of his kids hugging a stranger dressed like a cute, moderately stoned alien. He thanked the opossum, shook the rhino's hand, then escorted his family back into the sweltering summer sun.

The pirate ride no longer held the same appeal.

"We're leaving," Janet yell-whispered into Bronski's ear, carting little Becky away toward the parking lot, Jeremy following in a half-daze at their heels, gnawing on his lollipop with sluggish bites. "You need to find us somewhere to sleep."

Bronski sighed. "I can do that," he replied, unlocking their rental minivan. The respirators were piled on the back seat, those empty plastic eyes staring back at Bronski from the upholstery as if he were the world's biggest idiot, as if he'd fallen for the oldest trick in the book.

"Great deal. Real great," he muttered as he pushed the masks onto the floor, making space so Jeremy could stretch out on the seat, the A/C breathing down from twin vents in the ceiling.

***

That night, they didn't return to the burnt floor. Instead, Bronski found a public park, one with a lot of trees. They'd sleep beneath the open sky, the far-off arches of the rollercoasters hidden by citrus groves and palms, the firework show muted by distance and several freeways.

They found a flat stretch of ground far enough from any wetlands. All the ponds and rivers in the area had signs warning of alligators, of water snakes, of parasitic fish. Bronski laid out blankets on a layer of mulch and drying fronds, smoothing out the pointed leaves before his family could take their place.

The night sky resembled the charred ceiling in some distant way, the eroding blackness of it, but each breath Bronski sucked down was light in his lungs, the synthetic plastic replaced by his wife and children's sweat, the fried chicken-finger scent clinging to their mouths.

"Are we going back for our stuff?" Jeremy asked, half-asleep.

"I'll go up and get the bags," Bronski said.

"That place smelled," Jeremy muttered, tucking his face into his mother's side.

Bronski could almost smell the smoke on the wind, but for the moment, the scent of char was far off, a concern for later. He sucked in another lungful of air and lay quiet, listening for something moving in the bushes, something from those warning signs with scales, sharp teeth, mouths that could easily fit a child. He'd stay awake all night if he had to. He'd been careless with his family's safety once.

WASH'ASHORE PLASTICS MUSEUM

From the dock, the sandbar across the bay looked awash with shipwreck survivors dragging themselves from the surf. It was low tide. The bay was a mirror of sky reflecting off the green Atlantic. Corin guided his Boston Whaler through the shallows, hoping to ferry the stranded back to shore. He'd already called 911 and the Coast Guard. Their nearest boat was an hour out.

It was mid-May. Salt spray kicked up from the boat's prow. As Corin approached, he noticed the bleached-white bodies were fixed in odd poses, hands on hips, rigid, fingers extended toward the sky. Some were inhumanly thin. Others were muscled like bodybuilders. Corin throttled down with the realization. They were mannequins, the same as any other debris ferried down the coast on the Gulf Stream.

Cutting the engine, he nosed into shore.

Corin gathered the mannequins like kindling, stacking each in the boat's bow. He returned for five trips. It was impossible to fit them all in one go. He couldn't leave any behind for someone else to mistake for disaster.

***

"What will you do with them?" the EMT asked, his ambulance parked on the overgrown lawn in front of the museum. The man had already radioed in to cancel the approaching rescue boats.

"Add them to the collection," Corin said, arranging mannequins outside the back door. "Not sure where they came from. They've got manufacturer's engravings on their heels, but I don't recognize the country, or city, or wherever it is."

"That's weird," the EMT replied. Every local knew what Corin did for work. "What's it say?"

"Made in Binnsend. Could be European or some place they colonized. That doesn't narrow it down much."

"Could you let me know when you figure it out?"

"Sure," Corin said, positioning the last mannequin in the sprawling crowd. There were over thirty. Corin couldn't fit them all in the showroom. The renovated cottage serving as Corin's Wash'ashore Plastics Museum was already cramped, the original pine flooring buckling under displays and dioramas. Every wall hung heavy with debris sifted from the surf.

Once the ambulance pulled away, Corin selected the least-worn mannequin and hefted it through the back door. Inside the museum, the air was cool. The cottage was built in the 1800s by his great-great-great-grandfather and always felt damp.

With the mannequin cradled under his arm, Corin moved through the display section, past objects that ran aground on nearby beaches. There were yellow rubber ducks and children's pastel-blue swimming pools, Halloween masks and comic book action figures, life vests, lipstick tubes, and an entire jar of plastic tampon applicators.

The more common detritus was heaped together in aesthetically arranged piles, color coordinated in a rainbow spectrum. The countless straws and plastic soda bottles, the jellyfish-like plastic bags and cigarette filters. He had constructed a Christmas tree out of buoys and fishing line, had built a human skeleton from discarded running shoes. People came for the oddities, but the everyday objects, paired with statistics, were the real educators. The back wall was painted with a mural of the globe. Red and blue arrows traced coastlines, marking major and minor currents. Beneath, he listed which carried the most plastic, which deposited the most on the ocean floor.

With his free hand, Corin opened the door to his workspace. A dim computer screen cast a glow around itself. The rest of the room was left in darkness. He stood the mannequin beside his crowded desk and flipped on the overheads. The room was nothing but metal shelves of organized plastic, all labeled and cataloged. A single desk stood at its center.

Corin typed the name *Binnsend* into the search bar. No accurate results appeared. Pieces on raising reptiles and reconnecting with lost friends filled the screen. He altered the search, adding country names and continents, plastic plants and manufacturing hubs. Still nothing. As he pulled a world atlas from his overflowing bookcases, his door flung open.

"Can I have one?" Beth asked.

"Not yet. I need to do research first," Corin replied, dropping the atlas.

"On all of them?"

"Well, yeah. Who knows if one's different from the rest."

Beth, Corin's wife, operated an art gallery on the far edge of the property. While Corin displayed statistics and educational warnings, Beth made plastic debris into art, mostly sculptures and mosaics constructed from single-use items and bottle caps. Occasionally she carved portraits into disposable cooler foam or Styrofoam take-out containers. Her jewelry sold well. She wore a pair of crescent moon earrings cut from an old flip phone. Her blonde hair was held back by a black bandana.

"Why? Are you afraid I'll get all the foot traffic?" Beth asked, leaning against the doorframe. It was their usual joke of feigned rivalry.

Nearly three times the number of visitors passed through the art gallery's doors each summer as they did Wash'ashore Plastic. Both had door counters in their entrance ways. There was no arguing attendance. Corin didn't debate reasons one was favored over the other. He knew people liked beauty, the clean aesthetic art brought to trash. His raw, almost unfathomable data turned viewers off. People didn't like to confront the problem they added to. People did like to buy bottle cap portraits and jellyfish statues. It funded the majority of the couples' joint venture.

"No. That's not it. If I break them up, who knows what I'll miss. The process should be easy. They've got manufacturer's marks. If you go and grind one down to make beer coasters, I could lose something," Corin said, flipping through the atlas. He ran his finger down the index at the back, searching for Binnsend. It wasn't listed amongst the B's.

"You really think one's going to be that important?" Beth asked. "I'll keep it intact and use it as a display."

"Please, just leave them where they are. I'll figure this out in a week. Two tops. After that, you can take as many as you want."

"Good. There's no way you'd fit them all in here anyway," Beth said, waving a hand toward the showroom.

"You never know, people might pay to look through the windows of a cabin stuffed with mannequins."

"Very voyeuristic."

"If it gets people talking, I'd be willing to show more than just mannequins," Corin joked.

"I don't think that would further the message you're going for, Corin."

"Hey, you never know," Corin said. "People love a good spectacle for the sake of distraction."

***

Corin was wrong. In a week, he uncovered little information on Binnsend. After two weeks, his notes were mostly blank, the few lines scribbled down crossed out in black pen. He spent his mornings researching the mannequins. Years ago, he would have been shellfishing at such an hour, but a slipped disc in his lower back forced early retirement. In the afternoon he acted as a docent in the museum, leading tourists through his displays, lingering before the current map, explaining how plastic affects the habitats of seahorses, turtles, and other marine life.

Corin traced his finger along the line for the Gulf Stream running up the Eastern Seaboard.

"The Gulf Stream deposits most of the plastic I scoop up, but the Labrador Current coming down from Greenland also plays a part," Corin said.

A little kid, tucked beneath his mother's arm, raised his hand.

"What can I do for you?" Corin asked with a smile.

"What about the other arrows?" the kid asked. "Where does their trash go?"

The map had over thirty currents outlined.

"Well, the simple answer is everywhere. Even though most of our plastic is carried by two currents, you also have the South Equatorial flowing into the Caribbean, then up around Florida. But it's possible for something to be dropped into the California Current and make its way here," Corin said, indicating several arrows moving along Antarctica and up the coast of Africa.

"So this stuff could come from anywhere?" the boy asked, pointing to the discarded shoe skeleton.

"Basically, yes. Every year eight million tons of plastic makes its way into the ocean. It comes from every continent. Most are single-use items only used for a few minutes before being thrown away," Corin said, reciting his environmental pitch. "That's why it's important we move away from using things like plastic forks or disposable coffee cups. We use them for a minute, then they clog our waters forever. Doesn't seem worth it."

The young boy nodded enthusiastically as his mother tucked a ninety-nine-cent coffee behind her back.

The group of tourists thanked Corin after he answered a question about a giant plastic squid that floundered ashore from Japan, then moved off on their own, inspecting other plastic oddities. While Corin stood next to the entrance, waiting for a hoped-for follow-up, the door opened, nearly catching his shoulder. Beth burst in, dirty blonde hair flowing behind her. An outrageous necklace made of braided fishing line and dulled fishing hooks clinked around her neck.

"You need to look at this," she said, lassoing an arm around Corin's waist, dragging him toward the door.

"I've got visitors," he said, gesturing to the tourists.

"They're not going to steal anything," Beth replied, pulling harder.

"What if they have questions?"

Beth looked over the people standing around the glass display cases. "Does anyone have any final questions?"

A chorus of *Nopes* and *All sets* greeted her.

Corin let Beth escort him out of the room, into the early summer air. The humid season was just beginning. She led him across the grass dividing her gallery from his museum, toward the water. The two buildings sat on a clear-cut hill that dropped down to a rock-strewn beach and the dock where Corin's boat was moored. It was low tide again. The smell of swamp gases and decaying marine life rose on the wind. She refused to tell him what she had seen as they walked.

"Tell me it's a mermaid," Corin said.

"Don't be a perv," Beth replied, whacking his arm.

As they drew near, Corin could see that it wasn't a mermaid, or anything else he hoped for. The bleached bodies of another twenty mannequins crowded the same sandbar as before. Their poses were different, less laid back and casual, more aggressive in their gesticulations. As Beth's sandals flapped against the dock's damp boards, he noted flexed arms and running strides half-submerged in sand. They paused at the end of the dock, squinting into the sunlight reflecting in silver crescents off the waves.

"Since I found them first, I get one," Beth said.

"Fine. You're helping me move them though," Corin replied, descending into his Boston Whaler. The boat rocked under his weight.

"Why didn't these show up with the first load?" Beth asked, unfastening the mooring lines.

"There's a million possibilities. Maybe some got snagged somewhere. Maybe they fell into the ocean later. Maybe someone's messing with me. Take your pick," Corin said, starting the engine.

"Hopefully it's not the last one," Beth called over the motor. She joined him on the boat's deck, sitting on the bench spanning the middle of the fiberglass hull. Corin brought the boat to full throttle and skipped along the shallows. The water at low tide was no deeper than five feet. It took less than a minute to nose onto the bar's sandy edge.

Together they filled the boat with mannequins, fighting the muddy suck of sand while loosening their bodies from the ground. The first thing Corin did when he laid a mannequin down was check its heel. On each, he found the engraving *Made in Binnsend*.

"I want this one," Beth said, holding up a female mannequin, her hands on her hips, leaning forward as if questioning an audience.

"Works for me," Corin replied. "She's all yours."

With the last of the mannequins loaded onto the boat, Corin helped Beth settle down into a nest of plastic limbs. He pushed them off the bar, soaking the edge of his shorts, before heading back to the dock. He'd have to add the new arrivals to the pale throng behind the museum. There wasn't much room left before they spilled around the corner, coming into view from the parking lot. He didn't want that. Didn't want questions without answers. Beth's mannequin lay across her lap. *One less I have to store*, Corin thought. He contemplated offering up more, but couldn't stand the idea of handing over a crucial subject.

***

Every morning, before opening Wash'ashore's doors, Corin went down to the dock to check if more mannequins washed up during the night. He thought of the trips as a way to clear his head before research. A few minutes alone in nature, the lap of waves, the flutter of birds skimming the shallows. Some days he found nothing. On others, he found entire mannequin families beached on the sand bar. Occasionally, a single white hand would emerge from the surf, but the bodies usually arrived in groups. Corin felt he was spending more time retrieving their bodies than researching them. The bulging disc in his back ached. Over the next month, he added fifty-three mannequins to the herd behind the museum. It was impossible to shield them from the public who flocked to the arrangement of barnacle-crusted models. Corin made up a sign. It looked the same as the others posted around the museum. It read: *Mannequins. Unknown Origin.*

The questions he feared came in every day. He gave the same answers.

"Still haven't found the place," he'd say to tourists and locals. "Come back next week. Maybe I'll have a better idea then."

And they did come back. People visited the museum in record numbers to view the mannequins. Local news channels ran Corin's story. The papers interviewed other experts on plastics and ocean currents. None of them could offer further answers, which only brought more viewers from neighboring states.

"Maybe I shouldn't find the answer," Corin said to Beth over dinner one night.

She laughed. "That would literally annoy you until you die."

"I know. I just can't believe I haven't found anything. I've emailed college professors and librarians, map makers, and archivists. No one's heard of the place. I'm starting to think it doesn't exist."

"Or maybe they're from more than one place, you know, Frankensteined together," Beth offered, cutting into her veggie burger.

"Still doesn't explain the manufacturer's mark."

***

"Have you ever seen anything like this before?" Corin asked a professor from Harvard visiting the museum. He asked the same questions of everyone with a remotely scientific background: faculty from UMass, geographers from Syracuse who stepped through the museum's door, molecular engineers. *Ever heard of Binnsend? Have you ever located an unknown territory? Have you seen this mark before?*

Corin arranged the mannequins around the museum's front lawn, some in clusters, others by themselves. They looked deep in conversation, laughing over a shared joke, ranting to the sky, pleading with those around to listen. Some seemed joyous in the tilt of their spine. Others looked pained from the slant of their shoulders. Two lay on the ground, their legs eaten out from beneath them by jetty rocks or the ocean floor. Families moved through the exhibit, examining their bleached pigment. Corin left one laying on a table, heel raised so people could see the markings on the foot. *Binnsend.*

"Sounds like an old English industrial town," said a freckled woman from Oxford. "That's not it though. Not quite. Binnend. It's missing the S. It was an old oil town that went under. Lots of refineries, but no production factories. I think it might have fallen into the sea."

The professor pointed to the region of England where the town once stood on the display map. Of course Corin had heard of the place. It came up in every search result, but the woman was the first to note it. He'd researched the town for weeks, searching for mentions of mannequin factories, or any sort of factory for that matter, inside the town. No matter how much he wanted it to be the place, there was nothing. It hadn't been misspelled.

"Did she find your town?" Beth asked after the woman and her family left.

"Close but no cigar," Corin replied.

"Sorry to hear that. How many did you add today?" Beth asked, helping Corin move a pair of muscle-bound mannequins to the edge of the display.

"Fifteen."

"How's it possible they keep showing up and no one's heard of this place?"

"Well, something is manufactured in India, stitched together in Taiwan, sent to Moldova to be dyed, then passed along to Spain for packaging. Maybe Binnsend is somewhere in between like you said, some stop we haven't heard of."

Corin imagined the sunken city of Binnend, Atlantis-like beneath the waves. Rows of barnacle-stuck factories churned out endless plastic bodies, the continual grind of cogs and gears unaffected by submergence. Waterlogged houses were plastered with seaweed and six-pack racks alike, families of crabs hunkering in eaves. Their rusting infrastructure was so congested with trash that sank from above, odd aquatic survivors sought revenge, letting their own manufactured junk float to land, to remind everyone of who they had been, the mistakes they made and continued making.

But Corin's waking dreams were rarely accurate.

Corin knew there were probably books he couldn't acquire and experts he couldn't contact on the subject. His resources had been exhausted. He'd traced everything from Nikes to life-size Dracula figurines.

Only the mannequins defied identification. Their bodies arranged along the unkempt lawn mirrored the statistics he taught on tours, their overwhelming presence a visual interpretation of the tons of plastic collecting in ocean gyres.

"It's like I said. You should never rule out a possibility," Beth added. "That's how I make art. Endless possibilities. Otherwise, you're restricted and everything becomes contrived."

"You're right," Corin replied. "I have no idea where these things come from."

"What do you think of this?" Beth asked, stepping aside from a pairing of mannequins she manipulated. They were sensually bent together, hips interlocked, pelvises brushing. Next to them, on the lawn nearby, she laid a baby mannequin, one of the more recent additions to the collection.

"Plastic begets plastic?"

"Good title. We can work with that."

"A little crass though."

"People like crass" she replied, stepping away from her work.

***

Corin guided his Boston Whaler on its usual route from dock to sandbar. He could see through the dissipating mist only four mannequins hung up that morning. *Thank God,* he muttered, rubbing his lower back. The day before it had been forty-three. The largest gathering yet. Some of them had been odd; extra limbs, a third arm, two heads, tails and wings, mythic appendages he could barely fathom. He piled the four relatively normal mannequins in the boat's bow. One had a stunted arm, but that was tame compared to the previous collection.

He headed the boat upwind, cutting through the surf.

Corin hauled the bodies up the slope toward the museum, which was now completely ringed by the bleached models, naked in the early morning fog. They resembled photographs of galaxies, each body a star orbiting the central hub of the building, the building few people entered anymore. They only came for the mannequins, their own likenesses reflected in the thousands, strewn about, representations of what they didn't want to acknowledge in themselves, but couldn't ignore any longer.

The mannequins were only there because people wanted to see them, wanted them to exist. They were like the other garbage people subsisted on, the tenth pair of running shoes, the seven straws to match their seven drinks at the bar, iPhone packaging. Part of Corin wondered if it was their desire that dragged the mannequins out of the ocean. Part of him still hoped there was a place on a forgotten map somewhere called Binnsend, the sunken city ever churning.

He continued to ask visitors if they'd heard of the country, but their answers never changed.

He was surprised to find an ambulance parked at the top of the grassy incline, idling, the lights mute. The blue uniformed EMT he had met when he first mistook the mannequins for drowning victims moved through the gathered forms. Corin figured another false alarm had brought the paramedic away from the station.

The man stopped here and there, noting arrangements, laughing at the sexual couple, the onlooker turning away from the ranting preacher.

"So, did you find an answer?" the EMT asked Corin after he offloaded the newest acquisitions.

"No. I mean, if you pulled out a map, I can't point to a specific place," Corin replied.

"That's surprising."

"Yeah, I was pretty disappointed at first, but I've gotten used to the idea of not knowing."

"Well, at least they aren't in the ocean anymore."

"There's always that."

The EMT nodded, checked the radio clipped to his belt, and looked off across the field of mannequins.

"Do you mind if I look around for a bit even though you're closed?" the EMT asked.

"No worries," Corin replied. "It's not like you're disturbing anyone. Spend the day, or come back tomorrow, or the next day. I'm sure more will show up."

"Hope you don't run out of space," the EMT said, walking off through the naked bodies. He was the only dark shape among the white models, pausing momentarily to admire their design, before moving off across the hill. The edge of the group was still far off beyond the museum, bodies drifting back toward the water and the endless pull of the current and the sandbar beyond, empty for the moment.

Corin doubted that would last long.

GROWTH/DECAY

Wren pasted flowers snipped from botanical texts to a blank canvas. She used her thumbnail to flatten daylilies in place. Green leaves ringed the white background in a wreath-like pattern. Sunflowers and rose petals erupted at its core.

There wasn't enough light in her apartment to actually grow anything. There were only three windows, each facing north, each facing a brick wall across a narrow alley. The few plants she had attempted withered and died. Their browned stalks littered her windowsills like a wall of the undead in an apocalyptic movie, decaying bodies only shaking when a wind swept through. She told herself she was going to stick to their paper counterparts.

Wren had to find beauty somewhere.

***

"Have you thought about grow lights?" Wren's latest Tinder date asked. He stood naked, paunchy and white, peering down at the plant husks. They had just finished having sex and were about to shower. She stood behind him, two clean towels slung over her bare shoulder above the tattoo of a blooming lady slipper, her brown hair held back by a scrunchy.

"It never crossed my mind," Wren replied, tossing the towels into the bathroom. The apartment had only three small rooms. It didn't take much effort to cross from one to the next.

"They're pretty straight forward. You could hang a bank of them from the ceiling, or get the smaller painter's lamp versions. Have you seen those? They have the little clamps that you can attach to anything," the guy said.

"Would you help me install them?" Wren asked.

The man hesitated, rubbing a hand over his shoulder, eyes on the ceiling as if he were scrolling through his mental calendar.

"Maybe?" he replied, before stepping into the blue-tiled bathroom and turning the shower handle, summoning a downpour.

***

The guy never returned Wren's calls. Men she met online were always doing that. Once the sex was done and the prospect of deeper connection, or manual labor, reared its head, they were suddenly more focused on studying for the GREs or getting their plumbing license.

It didn't matter. Wren researched the lights, contacting the hydroponic shop three towns over. They set aside two banks of LEDs, their wavelengths dialed for the best grow pattern.

***

The store was awash in electric-blue. Strips of lights hovered over what looked like fish tanks full of vegetables. The entire room was warm and smelled of tomato leaves.

"So these are just for house plants?" the guy at the front counter asked. "This is Massachusetts. You can tell me if it's for weed, because if it is, you're going to want..."

"Nope. Just flowers. Flowering trees. Flowering shrubs. Anything flowering," Wren replied.

"That's completely cool. Just be careful with what species you grow. Some can be pretty demanding."

"I'll do my research," she said, picking up the lights.

***

Wren screwed four stainless-steel hooks into her ceiling, spaced far enough apart so they wouldn't swing into one another. The landlord would be pissed, but she figured she could learn to spackle the holes in the sheetrock. Everything was on YouTube.

Wren looped lengths of chain through both hooks so she could raise and lower the lights as the plants grew, adjusting for their height. She placed a long table made of cheap particle board beneath, a fixture she'd found on the curb after the local college let out for summer. It was warped, but she figured with the amount of water she'd be spilling on it, warping was inevitable.

She sowed a variety of seeds into pots and trays, bee balm and geraniums, lily and primrose. Chamomile for tea. Lavender for cleansing sprays. She wished she could grow lady slippers, but she read the pink flowers were impossible to propagate indoors.

Instead, she purchased established plants for the sake of time, the red dish of the hibiscus flower her favorite among them. She detailed a watering schedule in a notebook, marking how many weeks before each needed liquid fertilizer. The lights ran into timers set to mimic sunrise and sunset. The whole thing was a sprawling science experiment, an artificial world. The scent of potting soil grew thick in her condensed rooms.

***

The guy who suggested she get the grow lamps tried to parlay installation into another date a few weeks later. Wren sent back an image of her set up, the green necks of seedlings crawling through the soil. She didn't add any words. He didn't write back. Wren was glad he could take the hint. She'd been ignoring her online dating profiles after the twin improvised suns began burning beneath her roof. There was only so much she could focus on in her days between work and growing. One more disappointing romance wasn't going to improve anything.

***

Wren had been using online dating apps for three years. She'd lost count of the number of dates she'd been on. Several had spawned months' long relationships, but rarely did they churn into something greater. She found a startling number of people lied in their profiles. Occasionally it was something negligible, like stating they'd read a book they hadn't. Sometimes it was something ridiculous like their height. One guy claimed to be six-one when in reality he was five-seven. Wren wasn't bothered by the height. She had no problems with tall guys or short guys. She had a problem with someone lying about something so impossible to miss. If they lied about the obvious, what about everything else?

Honesty meant a lot to Wren. She hadn't lied in her profile. Five-four. Average weight. A degree in studio art with its residual debt. A love for fairytales. Cat allergies. A lapsed tennis practice. A few tattoos.

Truth wasn't difficult for her.

Why did it have to be for everyone else?

Something similar always happened after the first few dates. Some divergence would separate the written life from the lived. A dislike of animals. A heavy drinking habit. Anti-vaxxer tendencies, seatbelt-free driving preferences. A kink that was a little outside her comfort zone.

So many times the professed poets hadn't jotted a word since freshmen year writing. Many of the screenwriters were just guys who wanted an excuse to watch movies. Painters often preferred Instagram. The gym rats were generally honest about the time spent lifting weights, but that was about all they did, and that wasn't what Wren was looking for.

Just someone who was kind, truthful, and preferably had a green thumb. Or desired a green thumb.

There was always space to learn.

***

It took a month before her flowers began to blossom. Most were suspended from spindly stalks, their colorful faces broad beneath the light. Wren had honed every detail of growth, had read guides on each flower, customizing water levels accordingly, fertilizing frequency and humidity preferences. It seemed more simple than she expected. There was no magic needed to call the sprouts forth, no ritual or ancient word that would unfurl a bloom. Blood sacrifices weren't needed.

And that made her a little disappointed.

***

After her shift at the print shop one day, fingers tinted blue from ink, she paused on her walk home, noticing a pink lady slipper probing through the duff layer of a stretch of forest between two houses. Their city was an odd mix of suburbia, rural, and old mill town brickwork. The common combination for Western Massachusetts.

It was her favorite flower. How could she not stop?

Wren bent to examine the swollen bell of its petals, the sensual hints of its shape. She'd read about their endangered status, their difficulty in domestication. So much relied on fungal presence and decaying soil.

Wren marked the spot on Google Maps, telling herself it would be better to return at night. She'd never heard of someone being arrested for harvesting endangered plants, but she didn't want to find out if it actually happened.

She liked the idea of a challenge, proving those articles wrong.

***

That night, she crept back to the spot. She wore all black, carrying a small pot stuffed with soil and a steel trowel. The road was dead. No headlights blared across the oak trunks. No footsteps snapped dried twigs on the jogging path cutting through the undergrowth.

Wren bent to her work, gently digging the trowel around the flower's root system, extracting it with delicate fingers. She eased the growth into the pot, settling the new soil around its base.

As she tamped around the stalk with her fingertips, a faint whisper crawled between the trees, laughter, a sprawling chorus of pinprick voices. Wren looked deeper into the woods, searching for a children's choir or some nightmare wind chimes, but there was nothing, just bending branches swaying in the breeze.

She didn't wait around, having read enough fairytales to know the next scene might not be so placid.

***

The lady slipper should have shriveled within two months. That was the extent of its typical bloom. Fall was setting in and the plump magenta veins running through the bell still swelled full. Between its harvest and present, she'd gone back to the woods, snatching other native species of tree and shrub from the leaf litter, transplanting them into pots, arranging her own tiny forest beneath the artificial suns. Online forums said the plants wouldn't like the seasonless existence, but none had begun to brown.

***

"Any new boys?" her mother asked over their weekly phone call.

"Let's call them men, for both of our sakes, and no, no men. I've been busy," Wren replied.

"With work?"

"Not really."

"Are you reading too much again."

"No more than usual," Wren replied, toeing a collection of folklore at the end of her bed.

"Your gardening can't take up that much time."

Her mother had hired a crew of men to mow their lawn and trim their hedges for Wren's entire life. She was pretty sure the woman didn't understand basic botany.

"You'd be surprised."

"Well, that's all well and good, but aren't you lonely? Living alone isn't easy. I remember when I was your age, before your father came along. I never liked the nights. The cold. The..."

"I'm actually less lonely now, if I'm being honest."

"How?"

Wren didn't reply.

The world had shrunk in some way. Wren didn't miss faces staring up at her from her phone, the potential each possessed. She didn't miss the guessing game, the fact-checking she'd do as she scrolled through their attributes, their likes and dislikes, attempting to intuit if he'd be able to hold a conversation, if he'd spend the entire date staring at her boobs.

With plants, she understood what she was getting. There was a direct set of laws governing their lives, a concrete combination of factors to keep them in bloom.

"Are you okay, honey?" her mother asked after the pause.

"Totally fine, Mom. I'll send you a few pictures when my new additions open up next week."

***

Wren scavenged a mountain reserve in Holyoke, sweeping off trail to see what fall had summoned. Aster were in flower. Their purple-wreathed petals were stark against the autumnal background. It was near sunset. The lake to her left reflected the fading orb.

Running her hands through the soil around a flush of flowers, she felt something solid rap her shoulder. She swore in her mind, assuming it was a park ranger, reminding her that nothing on the property belonged to her, that the flowers were best left in their native habitat. Aster weren't endangered, so at least there was that.

Wren turned.

No uniformed guard hovered behind her.

No one did.

"I'm not a fan of lurking weirdos. If someone's out there behind a tree, I'm not afraid to stab you," she said, gesturing with the trowel.

"Hiding behind isn't the right way to look at it," came a voice that was a dozen voices and a singular note at once.

Wren looked around, searching for the speaker.

"Your eyesight is poor," the voices replied.

"That's not what my doctor says."

"They lie sometimes."

"I won't argue with you there."

Wren pushed aside the limbs of a pine, searching for the dozen bodies that had to be hidden nearby. She did the same to a cluster of ferns, then the thorny protrusions of a holly bush.

"We have a proposition," the choir of voices intoned, resonating from the spot she had just stood. There was no way she'd missed someone standing there. The voices emanated from the trees, or something inside she couldn't see.

"I won't let you use my body for compost, if that's what you're getting at."

Wren had read enough fairytales to know the typical tricks ancient oaken fathers would play, the sacrifices they tried to coax from young women and boys, acorns buried in throats and chest cavities, sprawling tendrils drifting from mouths, searching for open sky.

"You are better with growth than decay," the voices replied.

They seemed to swell from each tree in the vicinity, hollowed out and resonant like the body of a cello.

"And how do you know that?" Wren asked, brandishing her trowel.

"You have a window. Our siblings are tall."

"That's creepy."

"We assure you we've ignored all the other unfortunate goings-on within your residence..."

Before the voice concluded, Wren ran, her flannel jacket billowing behind her as she ducked around limbs and trunks. She had also read enough to know that nature angered was never a good thing. Skeletons stripped to the bone by pitchy fingers, corpses hung in over-laden boughs. She didn't want to fill that role, so she darted away. The voices didn't follow. Trees didn't bend to block her path as Disney would have them do.

***

When she got home, Wren put her ear close to her recent transplants, letting their leafy limbs tickle her neck. She searched for the voice, the relation to the sentient presence she'd met in the forest. She couldn't help personifying the little seedlings, imagining a babbling version of the old trees' words. They were young, of course they didn't have the vocabulary to express their dismay.

The potted flowers and saplings were silent.

Wren dragged her blinds closed, noting an ancient elm looming over a house three doors down. She didn't need any more reports filtering back to the glade in Holyoke.

***

For the first time in months, Wren revisited her dating apps. Fear of the woods and the loneliness of an empty bed guided her fingertips. Hundreds of notifications filled her DMs. Most were just guys saying *Hey*, or *Hey Grrl*, or *Watcha doin*. There were a few dick pics and eggplant emojis. She deleted each unsatisfying appeal until she alighted on a paragraph-long message from a guy named Stan. He managed proper punctuation. He mentioned several specific things from her profile: her love for animated movies, post-rock, and herb gardens. He ended it with a corny joke about *Little Red Riding Hood*, Wren's least favorite fairytale, but she let that slide. She wanted to give things another try. If she was going to have a horde of enlivened oaks pawing at her over a hobby, she didn't know if it was wise to continue said hobby.

***

Stan beat her to the sushi restaurant. He got them a table by the window overlooking Main Street and all the other eclectic eateries there. He had curly hair, a narrow face, and a jaw that was pronounced but somehow soft. He wore a denim shirt and a pair of tight tan pants. A tasteful sparrow tattoo fluttered on his forearm.

"I ordered us some squid. I hope you don't mind," he said as she took her seat.

She wasn't late. She wondered how long he'd been sitting there.

"Totally cool with me," she replied, guessing he was the kind of guy that would pick up the tab.

"I love squid. I feel a little bad eating them sometimes, given their intelligence, but I figure if they were really smart, we wouldn't be able to catch them, right?"

Wren forced a laugh. The joke was more disturbing than genuine. She never wanted to be thinking of her meal's mental capacity before she skewered it with a fork.

"Everything's got to die sometime," Wren replied, spreading the napkin across her lap.

***

Their conversation moved forward in a predictable fashion. Questions about their past, what they studied in undergrad, siblings? no siblings? Wren wasn't feeling a spark, but she also wasn't feeling repulsed, which was more than she could say about most of her past dates. Stan seemed anxious. He was probably the type who would open up after date three, after he grew confident he wasn't going to mix up her name with his last girlfriend's.

"What makes you happy?" Stan asked after Wren popped a roe-covered salmon roll into her mouth.

"What?" she replied, the sharp inhale of wasabi climbing her sinuses.

"You know, what makes life fun? What do you look forward to?"

"Well, I grow things," she replied. "Mostly flowers, some trees. I get stuff from the forests around here when I can."

"That's cool. I tried growing mushrooms once, but only managed one flush."

"Like, psilocybin mushrooms?"

"No, they were shiitakes. The kind you get in the store. I fried them up with oil and salt and they were great. Psychedelics aren't really my thing."

***

She let him spend the night. They didn't have sex, but she let him wrap an arm around her as they slept, her in a long t-shirt, he in boxers. She'd forgotten how nice it felt to have warm skin against her own, something solid and breathing at her back. It had been months since she'd been close to another living being outside of the occasional brush with coworkers over the silk-screening press.

Maybe there could be a spark after all.

***

"Are you ever going to take me collecting?" Stan asked after date six.

They were sitting at a vegetarian restaurant across the street from the sushi restaurant. The city wasn't much of a city. Just one road lined with old factory buildings and storefronts, each renovated into hip coffee shops or bike co-ops. Stan touched the back of her hand as she stirred her miso soup.

"I haven't really been gathering new specimens," she replied. "You've seen how much space I have. There's hardly any room on the table."

The lie came naturally. She wasn't going to tell him some creepy Ent-thing had been watching her sleep. That wouldn't bode well for their subsequent dating potential. He'd already said he didn't enjoy psychedelics, and if they were watching her sleep, they were also watching him sleep.

"Maybe we could just go get a small one? Something that wouldn't take up much space. I keep picturing you, kneeling down in the leaves, uprooting some shrub, and it's kind of hot," Stan said.

"Hot in what sense? Like some sort of dirt fetish?"

"I don't think so," Stan replied, a blush pulsing over his cheeks. "I think I have more of a thing for that classic naturalist ensemble. You know, like a female Indiana Jones."

Wren wasn't going to correct him on the fact that he was an archeologist. She understood what he meant. She wondered if he was picturing her in one of those safari hats, the tan uniform, the only patch of color an ascot tied around her neck. She could get into it if that was his thing. Stan was a decent guy. Returned her phone calls. Brought her dinner after work. Spoke vaguely about science in an inquisitive, I-just-watched-a-nature-documentary sort of way. She wanted to keep him around.

"I could set that up if you want. I've heard it's easy to transplant stuff in early winter if the ground hasn't frozen," Wren replied.

"So that gives us, what? Like a week?"

"Sounds about right," Wren replied, picking up her miso soup and tipping it back into her mouth, swallowing the salty dregs at the bottom.

***

Stan wore a rain jacket over his wool sweater. Wren wore her most old-timey naturalist attire: a pair of black rain boots, a baseball cap, and a subdued poncho that looked more utilitarian than attractive. If she had more time, the costume would have been better. They'd parked by the Connecticut River, following a dirt road into the woods. They'd headed in the opposite direction from the Holyoke Range. Wren figured maybe the trees were different over there, less vocal.

"So what are we looking for?" Stan asked.

"They're called princess pines. They're not really a tree, but a club moss. They're pretty cute and really soft to the touch."

"And one of them will live fine on your table?"

"I think so. I haven't killed anything yet."

The lady slipper was still in bloom months after harvesting.

They walked beneath the arching branches of leafless oaks. The dirt road was washed out in sections, smoothed stones breaking through muddy sediment.

"What do you think about the idea of a green thumb? I mean, I totally get that you research the heck out of this stuff, but with the amount of things you're growing, I'd think at least one species wouldn't make it. It's almost magical, you know," Stan said.

"Well, I wouldn't be able to do it without the grow lights. Every old wives' tale has to originate in some truth though. So yeah, why not. Maybe green thumbs are an actual trait. Maybe some people are just born to raise plants. Maybe some people understand leaves and stems better than skin and bones," Wren replied, stepping from the road into the forest proper. There was a small glade of spruce circling around the green carpeting of a hundred princess pines. They huddled beneath her knees like a department store's Christmas display. She knelt beside them, placing her ceramic pot on the ground.

"Are you saying you understand the plant world better than the human world?" Stan asked.

"Something like that."

Wren looked over her shoulder, expecting to find Stan peering down at her work. After all, it was his inquisitiveness that brought her back to the forest. But he was still standing in the road.

"You're going to miss the whole process if you stay over there," she said, waving him to her side.

"I can see fine," he replied. "After all, you're just digging it up and sticking it in the pot, right?"

"I guess so," she said, disappointed he could reduce something so meaningful to such simplistic terms.

***

Stan stopped returning her calls. He neglected to get the tickets to *Cats: The Musical* he promised to take her to at the opera house. He hadn't been leaving his car in his usual spot two roads over from the public garage. Wren stopped by his apartment, a three-story walk-up perched atop a used bookstore and an ice cream shop. She rang the buzzer, but he neglected to unlock the door, or call down over the intercom. She didn't linger, feeling stupid standing next to the entrance to the ice cream shop mid-winter.

Wren hadn't been ghosted in almost a year.

She knew if she looked at her calendar, if she had been tracking the days, she would have noticed the correlation, the term limits of all her past relationships ebbing out at a similar point.

When Wren got home, she scrolled through the dating app where they met. Stan's profile was live again, or still live. She had never checked to see if he deactivated his account when they started getting serious. There was a warm tickle at the back of her throat, but she ignored it. Instead, she approached her miniature forest. She ran her fingers over thin branches, touching the soft curve of fledgling leaves.

Through the window at her back, she noticed the old elm, the way its gray skin dipped in the breeze.

She hadn't thought about the proposition since back in the fall. Hadn't considered what the trees had been offering.

Biting her lip, she picked up the first of the grow trays, carrying it down the back stairwell to her car.

***

"You brought all of them?" the voices intoned as Wren nestled each of her potted trees in the near frozen leaf litter. There were dwarfed species of maple and linden, a mulberry, and a few strains of wild grape. The princess pine she'd uprooted with Stan stood next to a willow she had no idea could thrive without its roots perpetually dipped in a stream. She arranged them like a summoning circle, concentric designs connecting one ceramic container with the next. She hoped it would bring her protection, or persuade the trees they didn't want to wear her skin like the skimpiest of capes.

"They're all here. I tipped a holly over on the car ride, but I think it's okay," she replied, pointing to the spiky ball of leaves.

"He'll bounce back," the trees replied.

"I wanted to hear the rest of your offer," Wren said, not wishing to prolong her anxiety. "I shouldn't have run away before I listened."

"Don't worry," the trees replied. "We usually get that. No one sticks around long after we open up."

"You and me both, buddy," Wren replied.

The trees laughed, leaves shivering and shushing. It didn't sound malicious. More sympathetic than anything. She had a feeling even the pulled blinds did little to stop their intrusion.

"We are always in need of someone to look after our young. Less and less of our children grow to maturity. It's hard to take care of them when you're rooted in place. They need more nutrients, someone to act as guard when those field trips of first graders come stomping along with their little clomping boots. Do you get what we're saying?"

"You want me to scrounge up some compost and scare kids away from the forest?"

"Yes, but not just kids. Also deer, and adult humans, and fire, if you can manage that. They're all terrible. Deer especially. They eat everything."

"And in return?"

"Stability. Companionship. Protection."

The entire glade drew near, bending close to hear Wren's reply. Shadows from their narrow, leafless branches stretched across her potted arrangement. The scent of pitch and pine needles was almost suffocating, the creak of bark and heartwood almost earsplitting. They were so close they seemed to create a cathedral over her head, a vast architectural monstrosity of liken-spotted skin, fractals forming windows into other worlds of verdant growth.

"I need something more precise," Wren replied. "Every time I don't get the specifics, I get screwed."

At that, all the trees straightened, the pale sky reappearing overhead, the other world receding into a divergent reality.

"We can do that," the voices replied. "No one's trying to trick you here."

***

Still interested in helping me with those lights? Wren texted the guy who'd ghosted her months before after they had sex. His pale, lumpy body came to mind, ghostlike beside the shower stall. She kept all the phone numbers of the men who'd disappointed her, kept the dating apps routinely updated. It was easier that way.

His reply was almost instantaneous. *Yeah, of course. Meet at your place?*

He inserted a winky face emoji directly after.

Actually, want to meet in the parking lot by Mt. Tom? We should go for a nature walk, she replied.

Oh, cool. I can do that. I love trees, the man responded.

Wren laughed, but didn't send the LOL through chat.

She stated the time to meet before shutting down her phone. She only charged it at the library every few days when she left the forest. She placed the phone into her pack leaning against the base of a maple. Her dirt-smeared shovel leaned above that, the bottle of chlorophyll nearby, a bandana looped about its neck.

She'd already dug the hole.

It was easier to do so beforehand, a lesson she learned the hard way. Stan's eyes remained open the entire time she removed the earth. If she wanted that judgment, she'd use the dating app for its intended purpose, but that was another life.

The trees needed nourishing, and she was the one with the green thumb.

EXOSKELETONS

1.

Lark shivered, wringing out the past hour's rain from his t-shirt. Gooseflesh rose along his thin arms as a breeze drifted down the path connecting the dump to the junkyard. He thought he had time before the storm clouds opened, but he was an entomologist, not a meteorologist. Things without exoskeletons never made much sense, which he believed partially accounted for why he lived in a pop-up camper. His renovated ranch had been more inviting. It sold quick after the divorce. The spare key still hung from a leather strap looped around his neck, along with the trailer's key. He had no doubt the new owners changed the locks, considering the recent newspaper articles with Lark's name in them.

Lark waded through the thick weeds and wildflowers obscuring the path to his trailer. After slipping the leather band from around his neck, he let himself in through the flimsy metal door. The room smelled like sweat-soaked sheets, cheap incense, and summer rain. On every window ledge stood glass dioramas of insects. Lark had assembled each, arranging the bugs in aesthetic poses so every joint and juncture could be easily examined. One ledge was covered in moths, simple gypsies, and sprawling green lunas. Next to them were the bees and wasps, gradually giving way to bluebottle flies and other Diptera. On the opposite side of the trailer, above the table that folded down into a bed, stood the beetles, fluorescent beneath the single bulb illuminating the space.

There were dragonflies, praying mantises, varieties of water bug and spider. The only species not in stock were butterflies. His ex-wife took them in the divorce settlement. *The only beautiful thing left*, he remembered her saying.

Lark bent down in front of the combination fridge/freezer beneath the sink. Opening the freezer door, he removed several glass vials with insects trapped inside. It was how he preserved them, the chill breath halting their decay without damaging their bodies. Even if the university wasn't going to fund his studies or pay for lectures, he would still gather specimens, not knowing what else to do with himself. It was the last remnant of his old life, a piece of himself preserved in amber.

He placed the seven vials on the countertop away from the dirty dishes and souring beer cans. Each held a single cicada. It was their year for rebirth, emerging from earthen wombs to pester the night with trilling songs. Lark had known if he didn't collect them, he'd have to wait another seventeen years before they returned. He had already picked out a glass case to arrange them in, a white foam backing in which to insert the pins. As Lark moved to uncap the vials, someone knocked at the door, causing him to nearly drop the glass.

Annoyed, he turned to find his aunt Jillian standing outside, a Styrofoam container in hand. Her husband, Bill, was the owner of the junkyard and the camper in which Lark now lived. Jillian had always been kind to him. She bought him books on insects as a kid, identification keys and trail guides to the local forests. Through the screened window, he could see her short gray hair brushed by the wind, her transition lenses dark in the afternoon light.

"It's open," Lark said.

Jillian turned the handle, letting herself in. She had to be in her seventies, Lark thought, unsure of her actual birthday. He felt bad that she walked through the junkyard to bring him dinner. He told her to call if she needed anything. It was easier for him to make the trek through the abandoned automobiles, dismantled motorcycles, and rusted-out school buses. She was on her second knee surgery.

"Bill ordered Chinese. I thought you might like some," Jillian said, placing the Styrofoam carton on the table, shaking rain droplets off her green jacket. She lowered herself onto the stiff cushioned bench on the far side of the table.

"Can I get you a beer?" Lark asked.

"Sure. Whatever you've got is fine," Jillian replied. "What are you working on?"

Her eyes focused on the cicadas. Lark picked one of the vials and handed it to her. Jillian turned the glass slowly, examining all angles as Lark cracked the cap off a bottle of Rolling Rock.

"I've never actually seen one of these up close. Only heard them at night," Jillian said, placing the specimen down on the counter. "What are you going to do with them?"

"I don't know. Preserve them. Take some notes. I figured I'd know when I got there," Lark replied.

"I know it's important that you keep up with your work, but don't you think we should start talking to one of those lawyers? See if we can get the accusations dropped so you can get your job back?" Jillian asked as Lark opened the container of Chinese food.

Fried rice and orange glazed chicken filled the room with the scent of grease and red peppers. He ate, thinking over her question. The things Harriet and his past students said to the papers were false, Lark reminded himself. The subsequent news articles and viral videos were worse. But there had been so much mania, so many speculations and untrue statements, he didn't know who would believe him. Jillian had given him a list of possible representatives a month ago, lawyers who practiced in slander and public defamation. He hadn't read over the names, contenting himself for the moment with the trivialities of his new job and the few specimens he gathered in the evening.

"I'm still thinking it over. I've got a lot on my mind right now," Lark replied.

"I know you do, honey," Jillian said, placing her hand on his. "I just don't want to see you get bogged down. You've worked too hard for this to ruin everything."

"It won't. I've read the list. I'm just making my choice. It takes time," Lark replied.

They spent the rest of Lark's meal discussing the cicadas and their role in deforestation, killing off weaker trees amidst hardier groves, sipping their sap dry. After a while, Jillian moved on to everyday minutia: how work was going, what Uncle Bill was restoring in his garage, opening night at the town fair. As Lark ate the last bite of chicken, he asked Jillian if his parents had sent him any mail. He had been calling them for weeks with no reply. After the allegations, they grew distant, eventually cutting off contact. Aunt Jillian was the only family member who continued to speak with him. Not even Uncle Bill said a word. He just grunted in Lark's direction before moving on with his day.

"Not yet," Jillian replied. "They'll come around."

"I don't know about that," Lark said, moving to the sink. He washed the remaining grease out of the Styrofoam container, then added it to a bin of non-recyclable material he gathered. The recycling center at the dump where he worked only took select types of plastic and glass, paper and cardboard. Styrofoam, along with a dozen other items, were thrown into the garbage when it arrived at the recycling center. Lark had been collecting it and cleaning it, telling himself he'd find a use for the materials, that someday the technology would exist to break it down into something less harmful to the environment.

"Can I keep one of these?" Jillian asked before leaving.

"I've got six others. Why not," Lark replied, pushing the glass vial across the table.

"Thanks," Jillian replied. "Promise me you'll pick a lawyer this week."

"Will do," Lark said, walking her to the door. "And thanks for dinner."

"You wouldn't have eaten otherwise."

Lark shrugged. Jillian pulled up her hood and stepped into the rain. The drops pattered on the metal roof, covering the sound of her footsteps as they receded through the tall grass.

***

He hadn't understood their bodies, Harriet and himself. How they moved. How they were meant to connect and glide in time. Their soft tissue and hidden bones were foreign in comparison to his studies. Less limbs. No segments. A lack of antenna. He knew every function of a dragonfly's mandible, every movement of a spider's spinneret, but the variations were alien to his own composition. When studying the human body, he grew lost, attempting to reconcile the two knowledge bases into one. Needless to say, the sex was awful. Communication skills were only slightly better. It didn't help that he refused new approaches, always looking to the insect world for answers. Damselflies adjoined themselves while flying pond to pond during mating season. Crickets sang vibrating songs with their legs to woo one another. He liked to ignore the fact praying mantises decapitated their males after courtship.

That's where the unraveling started. Harriet had asked Lark what he thought about when they had sex. *You don't communicate enough. You never tell me what you want or if you even like what I'm doing.* She didn't say this with malice, just inquisitively, with a touch of sadness. Lark hesitated with his answer, not wanting to tell her he imagined they were moths or grasshoppers or ants. What he said was, "Sometimes I think about bugs."

Harriet's lip curled in a shiver of disgust, which she attempted to mask with her hand, but Lark noticed. She smiled after and told him they would work on it. She tried to work on it for ten years. Even though he didn't tell her he was thinking about insects, they were still there, chirping their night melodies in the background when they made love. No matter what season, the crickets sawed away in the depths of his mind.

***

Empty glass bottles were arranged on a smooth, sun-bleached wooden table. Cardboard overflowed from a moveable metal bin carted away by eighteen-wheelers once a week. Newspapers, stacked in six-foot heaps, filled another storage trailer. A dozen plastic receptacles were huddled beneath the overhang where Lark stood, organizing plastic that townspeople couldn't place in the correctly labeled receptacles. He juggled Coke bottles, orange prescription jars, egg cartons, milk cartons, cartons for substances he had never heard of. The smell of the place was somewhere between sour milk, melting plastic, and gasoline vapors.

Zeke stood next to Lark beneath the overhang, leaning against the plywood walls, not doing much of anything.

"You know what my wife said?" Zeke began, starting another one of his stories that went nowhere. "She said we're going to have oceanfront property in twenty years, the way the sea's supposedly rising. Not saying I believe in that stuff. I haven't seen the proof myself but, God, would it be nice to see those waves outside my window. Hell, my property value would skyrocket."

"That's nice, Zeke," Lark replied as he tossed a yogurt container in the appropriate bin. "But I don't think they have definite figures as far as that goes. You live in a hollow, right?"

Zeke nodded in reply. "What's that got to do with it?"

"Nothing," Lark said. "Just wondering."

An elderly woman carrying a plastic bag filled with assorted recyclables walked up to them and handed off her trash, eyes hidden behind black lenses. Zeke told her they would take care of it, smiling. Then he handed the items to Lark.

"So what are you doing with all that stuff? Siding your place with it? Patching a leaky roof?" Zeke asked, one hand lolling over his paunchy shirt front. He was staring at the bag filled with Styrofoam and plastic detritus Lark collected that day. None of it was accepted at the recycling center.

"Nope. I've been gathering it to bring to another facility, one that accepts what we don't," Lark replied.

"They take all of that?" Zeke asked.

"Well, some of it."

"Aren't you a saint."

"I do what I can."

Zeke was the only other worker stationed at the recycling center. The other dump employees circled the premises in front-end loaders, flattening heaps of debris or operating the hydraulic press to cram household waste into tiny cubes shipped off each morning. Lark's eight-hour days were spent making up for Zeke's lack of motivation and rude mannerisms toward patrons.

"Any new bug facts today?" Zeke asked. Startled, Lark dumped half an unemptied carton of orange juice on his work shirt. The scent of moldy citrus flourished in a sudden gust, nearly overwhelming him as he wrung the foul liquid from the fabric. As he straightened himself, he searched his mind for something Zeke could hold onto, something to spark curiosity where there had been none.

"Do you know how many sexual partners a bee has throughout its life?" Lark asked.

"No idea. Seventeen?" Zeke replied.

"Up to fifty-three. What do you think of that?"

"I think if reincarnation is real, let me come back as a honeybee," Zeke replied with a laugh.

Lark was glad his companion was enthusiastic about learning. Which is why he neglected to mention it was only the female bees mating fifty-three times, and that once the males deposited their sperm, they died. He knew Zeke might change his mind if he heard the rest, so he kept it to himself as he flattened cardboard boxes to fit in the steel bin.

***

Lark kept textbooks he co-authored stacked in the corner of his borrowed trailer. On top sat a diorama of two Hercules beetles, horns locked in eternal conflict. Lark was known around campus for his Insects and Human Society class. Half of the freshmen during his tenure sat riveted through his lectures comparing beehives and ant colonies to large cities and government structures. At points, it sounded like science fiction, some horrific dystopia where mindless drones flit from one job to the next, living unexamined lives, subject to unseen voices guiding their steps. He always received excellent student-teacher evaluations. On RateMyProfessor, he even received a hundred or so ratings of *HOT*, in addition to the glowing reviews that plastered the feed.

The website removed his profile once the allegations began.

Lark didn't like to let himself linger on his life in academia. He let the layout of campus be replaced by the arrangement of the junkyard, the winding aisles of rusted pickup trucks and crumpled sedans. His spacious office had become a foldable table and an odd assortment of specimens crammed onto thin ledges. Despite the list of lawyers Aunt Jillian had compiled and her kind words, Lark doubted anything would change. His colleagues refused to return his emails. The publishing house set to print his latest findings canceled the release, requesting their advance be returned. Lark had done so. He was blacklisted, and in a field as competitive as his, there were a hundred other drones in line, half a dozen syllabi already drafted for next semester.

He found himself watching dragonflies flit about outside his windows, dipping into a cloud of male mosquitoes. Lark knew the rate at which their wings vibrated, the amount of prey they consumed in an evening. Part of him wanted to shed his skin to become like them: light and agile, ferried about by the currents of the wind, ravenous. But instead, he was stuck in a clumsy composition of flesh, ill-articulated and flawed.

He went back to the recyclables he had been cleaning in the sink, spraying dish soap on his flaking sponge. Heaps of detritus were piling up about the camper: the Styrofoam boxes, plastic bags, odd bottles and cans that were only accepted in Maine or Hawaii. Even though the dump did collect newspapers to be pulped, Lark couldn't let those that contained his story go. Whenever he stumbled across one at work, he would secret it away, somehow protecting himself from further accusations. They stood in a heap next to the textbooks, neatly piled in a straight tower. Harriet always looked so good in the photos. Blonde hair pulled back in a long braid. Her thin nose and narrow jaw giving her the look of an elf from fantasy RPGs, which was coincidently how they met.

He had been the Dungeon Master for their high school *Dungeons and Dragons* group. Harriet, with her thick braces and acne-covered cheeks, was an elvish mage. The campaigns he designed grew more elaborate, the stories more vivid with each meeting, all in an attempt to woo her. He incorporated her favorite geographic landmark, hot springs, into every hand-drawn map. The bosses coincidentally had similar names to the girls that bullied her in school. She finally asked him out after a long trek through a haunted woods where the ghost of Jerome Salinger, the creepy math teacher who always hit on Harriet in B block, was buried. Lark could barely reply, his tongue turned to joyous stone. The years leading up to college were amazing for him: fantasy and sci fi romance unwinding on his twin-sized mattress.

College was similar, except for the queen-size upgrade in their first shared apartment. But in grad school, latent OCD blossomed, dividing his time between biology and love. Thinking back, Lark was surprised their marriage lasted more than ten years. She should have dumped him when he started disappearing for months on university-funded research trips. But the lies and slander, that was something he could never imagine coming from Harriet's lips. He had made mistakes, he wouldn't deny that, but she let her own fears carry her away. Infidelity and distance morphing into claims of sexual misconduct and grave robbing. Yet, Lark could barely find any anger to deposit on her shoulders.

"Are you alright?" Aunt Jillian asked from behind him. Lark threw the half-filled plastic bottle he had been washing into the air, soaking the opposite wall. He turned to find his aunt seated at the table, a glass bowl of homemade kale soup in front of her. It had been two weeks since her last visit.

"How long have you been there?" Lark asked.

"A minute or two. I didn't want to interrupt. Not really sure what you were doing though," she replied.

Lark couldn't bring himself to tell her he was daydreaming about his ex-wife and the life he missed.

"Just washing recyclables," Lark replied.

Aunt Jillian looked at the heaps of junk splayed across the countertops. The sea of plastic debris washed across his bed. In every corner lay twists of plastic bags knotted together from careless placement. Models of Styrofoam cities were erected on the built-in wall couch. She had to kick a dozen aluminum cans from her path just to get to the table. Lark followed her gaze as it moved from one mess to the next.

"I know. I'll take care of it. I'm going to borrow Zeke's truck tomorrow and take these up to the plant in Plymouth. They recycle this stuff," Lark said.

"Good, I'm glad. Your uncle's been worried about you," Jillian said.

Lark knew "about you" really meant "about the trailer," but he kept it to himself.

"That's nice of him," Lark replied.

"Well, in a way...it's more than that unfortunately. He wants you to move out and go into an in-patient program. There's one out in Western Mass, he said he'd be glad to cover the costs. I've seen pictures. It's nice. Not like what they used to be," Jillian said.

"I called those lawyers you told me about. They just haven't gotten back to me yet," Lark said.

"It's not that, Lark..."

"No, I'll do it. I'll take it seriously this time. You know how hard it's been. Can't you push it off for another month? I'll be back on my feet and things can move forward."

"Lark, please. I don't think you really understand how this is affecting you. How much do you weigh right now? A hundred and ten pounds?"

Lark hadn't thought about the size of his wrists, the way his joints protruded and pressed taut against his clinging skin. The outline of his ribcage was clearly visible through his thin t-shirt. There wasn't a mirror in the trailer, so he caught glimpses in car windows and grease puddles. He'd been feeling well though, his bones coming to the surface like the insects he studied. He felt closer to understanding some things that had slipped his mind before. In some way, he thought if Harriet were to take him back, he'd be able to see how they fit together. How their bodies could communicate.

"I couldn't tell you." Last time Lark checked, he weighed one-seventy.

"Your uncle says one week. I already had to argue with him to make it that long. I'm sorry..." Jillian said, tearing up.

Lark slid into the seat next to her, putting an arm around her shoulder.

"Hey, it's fine. If that's what Bill thinks is right, then I'll go. I can have this place cleaned up in a week. Like I said, Zeke's coming over with his truck tomorrow and we're taking it all away," Lark said.

Jillian sniffled, dragging a hand across her face, before prying the lid off the soup. She took a spoon out of the utensil basket by the window and stirred the dark liquid, bringing circular slices of sausage to the surface. The smell of kale reminded Lark of the days he spent at her house when he was a kid, rolling back rocks to find pill bugs beneath. They had laid together in tall grass by the vernal pool behind the house, watching dragonflies. Without saying anything, Lark found a clean bowl by the sink and a second spoon. He doled out a serving and left the other portion for his aunt. They sat next to each other, spooning the broth into their mouths, only occasionally making comments about the insect displays or how the cicadas seemed particularly quiet that evening.

2.

Zeke's dented pickup truck trundled through the narrow dirt lanes criss-crossing the junkyard. He followed Lark's instructions as he wound his way toward the back corner, past burnt-out minivans and jeeps sitting flat on the ground. The wildflowers that had proliferated a month before had lost most of their petals, only a few clinging to their summer colors. Zeke had to park a distance away from Lark's pop-up camper. The road evaporated into a sea of weeds and whatever lay beneath. Lark had warned about the broken windshields that hid like landmines. Zeke didn't want to puncture a tire, so he walked through the high grass, kicking at dandelion heads with the toe of his boot.

From a distance, Lark's camper looked like it had always been part of the landscape. Vines slithered out of the nearby forest and climbed up the sides. Small saplings sprung up through the trailer hitch. Moss and lichen created a second skin. Zeke made a joke to himself about the recycled plastic siding he mentioned a while back, how ridiculous it was to remove plastic from one recycling station to bring to another. Wasted gasoline outweighed the benefits. He never really thought of Lark as his friend. He'd been in rough shape though. Zeke couldn't help feeling bad, despite what the papers said.

At the door, Zeke knocked three times, the notes rattling in the thin metal frame. There was no movement through the screen window, no dark shadow shifting toward the entrance. He knocked again to no reply. Then he played with the handle, finding it unlocked. He let himself in.

At first, the place seemed like an image of the trash gyres in the middle of the ocean, all green and clear plastic swirling in a suspended vortex of water. But there was no water, and the center of the stationary vortex was a huge egg-shaped weave of recyclables. Zeke followed several plastic tendrils that stretched from each corner of the camper, holding the enormous chrysalis elevated off the floor. Plastic bags had been woven like ropes, intermeshed with newspapers and other paraphernalia. The center chamber, which would have been large enough to hold a person, was composed of Styrofoam packaging and odd bits of metal adhered to the seams. It looked like manic papier-mâché.

Zeke climbed the single step into the room, coming closer to the chrysalis.

The newspapers facing out toward him, blanketing vast swaths of the center chamber, seemed intentionally arranged. They were printed with headlines from Lark's fall from grace. Some, the earlier of the printings, mentioned accusations of relationships with students at the college where he taught. A pregnancy. Several pregnancies. Occult and disturbing sexual acts. Formicophilia, the ant farms he let crawl over their skin. There were shots of his wife in pantsuits, her makeup running down her cheeks and neck, pooling about her pronounced collarbones. All of the stories seemed to grow more wild as Zeke's eyes roved over the horrifying scrapbook. At some point, the infidelities were forgotten. In their place were notes about bizarre scientific studies, of bodies unearthed from nearby cemeteries to research the presence of insects in cadavers. Then the graves grew more recent. Family members of the deceased had given statements at the outrage of having their loved ones corrupted in such a way. *Monster* was printed in bold letters on nearly half the sheets. Zeke leaned in closer, searching for the sections dedicated to evidence, the pictures of the unearthed graves, of the bodies recovered from the supposed hidden shed in the woods. But he couldn't find any. Just quotes from offended witnesses.

In some places, the newspapers looked torn and altered, trimmed back to fit neatly around the chrysalis, sections removed or replaced, lines scribbled out in black ink. Part of him wondered if Lark intentionally obscured findings, if he wanted to keep a distance between the reader and the full account of his trespasses.

Zeke called Lark's name. He thought he heard something shift inside the chrysalis, but wasn't sure. "You in there, buddy?" he asked to no reply. *Why would a man do this?* he asked himself, thinking about serial killer movies he watched. Lark wasn't the kind of man he could imagine preying on women, dragging those bodies to his hidden study. But it was always the ones you least expected. Lark was a guy who talked about insects as if they were his children, who reprimanded Zeke whenever he moved to swat a bee.

Lark had once told him that caterpillars don't morph into butterflies the way everyone thought. Wings didn't sprout off their backs, legs extending, their waist growing narrow and aerodynamic. No, the caterpillars broke down into a mush of cells, slowly rebuilding themselves into something new, something better, no part of the old remaining.

As the thought crossed his mind, Zeke retraced his steps out of the trailer. Shudders spasmed through his lower back as he refused to look away from the chrysalis, all those crossed-out lines. His hand jutted out behind him, searching for the door.

Once outside, he closed the door, making sure the latch clicked into place before running to his truck. Throwing it in reverse, Zeke found a space between a beat-up VW Beetle and an old fishing boat to turn around, following the same roads he had taken to reach the deepest part of the junkyard.

In his hurry, a cloud of dragonflies and cicadas rose from the high grass, obscuring his vision in a fog of beating wings. When his wheels finally connected with pavement, only a singular moth remained trapped in the cab of his truck, bumping into the closed passenger window. Zeke hit the automatic switch at his elbow, forcing the glass to roll down. For a moment, the insect hovered there, brown wings outstretched. Then a gust from outside swept in, tugging the moth away into the truck's air stream.

Zeke closed the window so another couldn't take its place.

SOMETHING AQUATIC. SOMETHING HUNGRY.

The Misguided Merman lay on the quarried stone of the breakwater, orange hull tilted to the sky, rigging trailing into low-tide mud. A halo of gulls orbited. The smell of a weeks' old catch tainted the air. James recognized his uncle's fishing boat from a distance as he jogged near the wharf on Commercial Street in Provincetown, sweat slicking his t-shirt to his chest.

The boat had been missing for days. Local papers predicted engine failure or poor navigation. Rumors around town tended toward darker fare, most involving his uncle's barroom attendance and other habits not suitable for the morning news.

Everyone seemed to know his name, and not in a favorable sense.

The night before, James' aunt joked about etching *Lost at Sea* on a headstone. Half the grave markers in their family plot contained some variation of the epithet, had rough sailboats carved into granite, a number without bodies buried beneath.

Boats flung against the breakwater weren't uncommon. When weekend sailors mis-tied mooring lines or storms sheared cleats from rotting wood, another craft would hang up on the rocks. Even with the commonality, James knew something was off. Boats only arrived on the breakwater once they broke their moorings. *The Merman* had been out at sea for a week. Someone had to steer the ship around Long Point Light and into the harbor, otherwise the boat would have run aground near the sandy tip of Cape Cod.

James would have heard his uncle come in the night before if he'd made it to shore. The man was heavy on the stairs, never good at closing doors or oiling their hinges. James had rented a room from his uncle and aunt for two years, deciding whether to pursue the family business on the sea or to attend college. He'd loved the open air, the salt on his skin, all the unusual aquatic life they'd dredged up only for him to cast back into the sea, species absent from their trawling list. James hated the idea of waste, of needless death, unlike his uncle. Twenty percent of fish caught commercially were thrown back dead or alive based on regulations and quotas.

The more James read into it, the more disillusioned he became. For every sea robin he rescued, there'd be three dead. But the nets had been growing lighter with each trip. Predators had been getting better at snatching up hauls before they made it to the deck, tunas snapped off long lines, only heads and spines coming in with the hooks. James caught shadows beneath the surface, following the *Misguided Mermaid* in and out of the harbor, trailing them through open waters.

"It's just seals," his uncle had said without looking over the side.

"I don't think they like to go out this far from land," he replied.

"Think what you'd like. We're still losing fish."

"But..." James trailed off. He'd once looked up to his uncle, thought he knew everything about the sea, but he was continually reminded the only thing the man cared to know was profit margins, how to grow them, how to farm them, how to ignore every other harsh reality that came with his business model.

A BA in Computer Science or Botany was looking better and better with each passing day.

***

James had heard his aunt move out into the night around 3 a.m., returning just before dawn as he was getting ready to go for his morning jog. He knew she visited the docks, a lone watchman in the early morning gloom thanks to insomnia and the questions only brought about by darkness. She'd taken up the habit before the *Merman* went MIA, staring out over the blank ocean, searching for irregularities in the surf.

Over the past months, James' uncle had been coming home late, the scent of other women on his neck, his clothing: floral, sea salt, and ambergris. His aunt found it suffocating. Open air was a needed cleanse. They hadn't been in love for years. Economic dependence staved off divorce. Their mortgage principle wasn't getting much lower, credit card debt barely kept at bay.

There was always another poorly reasoned reason to stay.

Swallowing his gorge, James ran across the beach and traversed the rocks, fighting back the urge to vomit as he scaled the upended hull, fingers bloodied by outcroppings of barnacles. If his uncle was onboard, he'd need help. He imagined heart attacks, propeller lacerations, an arm caught in the winch. James couldn't wait for an ambulance. He knew CPR, how to tie a tourniquet. High school health class had taught him something.

He stumbled over the tilted deck, sidestepping coiled lines lying everywhere. One door to the below-deck cooler was open, the smell of rot breathing from the chasm.

The cockpit was empty. His uncle's favorite Red Sox cap hung from a mirror. A woman's lace bra dangled from the same fixture, seaweed stuck in the clasp. Beer bottles lay heaped in the corner. When the wind stirred, hollow notes rose from their open mouths, their glass sides shivering against one another.

His uncle and aunt had been deep in a feud the day he left. Another brawl over drinking habits and dwindling bank accounts. They never spoke of the women, where he spent his nights. That was never the primary concern. His uncle had left without him that morning, rage spurring his departure two hours before James' already early alarm went off

The fish had been moving farther and farther offshore with rising water temperatures. His uncle had to leave earlier and earlier each morning, even before anger issues flared. It wasn't an enjoyable way to live. Neither was being drunk more hours than not. It was a trend among locals, one of the reasons James' father moved to Maine to take up timber-framing, selling his boat and lobster pots before heading inland.

I'm not telling you how to live your life, but fish aren't always the best companions, he'd said the last time they spoke.

James was beginning to see what he meant.

***

The Merman seemed abandoned. James checked the storage lockers, which were empty. No one hid amongst the tackle. Nothing but loose wires dangled beneath the dashboard. Only gulls landed on the crosstree. A squall of birds drifted overhead as the wind changed direction, dragging with it the rotting scent from below, the tuneless moaning of the discarded bottles.

James circled back to the opened cooler, careful to avoid the lines draped everywhere. Peeling away the second door, he was greeted by a sea of blue-black fins, bloody scales, and the calf and thigh of a grown man, sickly white, severed at the hip.

James lost the battle against his stomach, adding its contents to what lay below.

He remained on his knees, wiping at his lips, as a shuffling at the stern called his attention. A woman stood there, sun low in the sky, a nearly translucent seafoam dress covering her frame. In her left hand was the skin of a seal, split down the middle, eyes empty and bottomless. Her right hand was coated in blood, fingernails tapered to sharp keratin tips. A crimson river ran down her chin, its tributaries speckling the fiberglass deck at her feet.

She sighed, then stepped over the gunnel, dress billowing behind her.

She looked over her shoulder once, before running down the length of the breakwater, feet slapping wet stone. A distance out, the woman leapt from the rocks, sinking into the sea where low tide depths dropped off. A blur of fabric and seal skin parted the green-black water. There was a single thrash: a foot, a fin, then stillness.

Only the droplets of blood were left to align James' shifting realities.

He stumbled off the boat, neglecting to call 911. Someone else would find *The Merman,* what lay in its hold. He wanted nothing to do with it, or his uncle, or the swimmer and her second skin. Romantic notions of the family business had bled out months ago. He couldn't lie to himself anymore. It was curse, not bounty. James wasn't going to be the one to help what swam beneath the surface, saving the unwanted from careless nets.

Fishing villages down the coast were being abandoned by the fish. Cod and haddock knew better than most of the inhabitants. The scent of death was in the water. James could smell it now, how it clung to his clothing, woven into his hair. Scientists said it was rising temperatures, algal blooms, overfishing, and nutrient dumps.

James wondered if something else affected those numbers.

Something aquatic.

Something hungry.

Something his uncle fancied for a time, before the relationship was no longer viable. *You eat when the meal's on the table,* he'd always said. James knew when fish were a scarce commodity, predators would look elsewhere for protein. First in their nets, then aboard the ships. How long before they climbed the docks or walked down the sidewalk of Commercial Street? It was basic biology, the need to eat, something James wouldn't forget in his new landlocked life of textbooks and midterms, far away from the sea and what now resided in the harbor.

He'd tell his aunt then pack his things.

He had a feeling she might already know. All those nights on the docks, the way the water grew translucent under a full moon. It was hard to imagine she could have missed the swimmer. More likely she had called to it, pointed it in the direction of easy prey. The cod weren't coming back and his uncle had a good life insurance policy.

Some fishermen knew where to cast their lines better than others.

DREDGING THE BAY

From the distorted shadow of the green-tinged cube ascending the water column, Ron could tell it was a washing machine. He leaned over the boat's transom, charting its progress. It was early May, the air starting to warm with summer's approach. Gulls circled overhead. In the distance, the harbor was full of fishing vessels and pleasure boats rocking on their moorings. The docks, farther off, were clustered with early-season tourists, cameras pointed out to sea. The salvage truck was parked at the bottom of the loading ramp, ready for their afternoon collection.

The hum of the winch's motor chittered over Ron's shoulder.

The line spooled upward.

Ron had organized the bay clean-up months back. The bottom was littered with debris, pollution adversely affecting shellfish populations. Before the area was settled, the mouth of the bay was choked with oysters. It was said someone could walk across the water on their shells, never getting wet. Ron saw the cleaning as his retirement project, a small way to give back to the community, never expecting others would volunteer. It had been two years since he gave up quahogging, his back no longer what it once was. He'd let his beard grow, his hair spun long.

"What number's that?" Kieron asked from where he stood by the winch, lever in hand.

"Number five," Ron replied.

"I'll mark it down when we get it on board," Kieron said as the washer parted the waves.

Kieron kept a log totaling the items they'd dragged from the bottom. Among the highlights were hull-scarred dinghies, engine blocks, TV sets, endless lobster traps, microwaves, propane tanks, and just about everything else costly to dispose of at the town dump. Some people preferred tossing them over the transom on moonless nights to paying the twenty-five-dollar fee.

Kieron was in his thirties, brown hair clipped low, forearm muscles thick from hours hauling nets. His last name belonged to half of the other town residents, their lineage snaking back to the early days of Wellfleet. Unfortunately, he hadn't inherited any of the land that came with the pedigree.

"You got this one, Ron?" Jeremy called from the helm.

"Yeah, I'll drag it over," Ron replied.

"Watch out for the barnacles this time," Jeremy called back.

Jeremy also had a name shared by many along the coast and also lacked the land occasionally given in a will. He was tall, red-haired and freckled, face drawn down in an arrow's point from his goatee.

Ron was at least twenty-five years older than either of them. He'd moved to the Cape thirty years ago. His last name didn't show up on road signs or plaques denoting conservation land like his friends, a fact that always made him feel distant.

Kieron killed the winch. The washing machine dangled out of the water, spinning suspended, grappling hook wedged deep into the metal. Ron reached the gaff out, attempting to drag the appliance over the deck.

"Open the door out there if you can," Jeremy called.

"What do you think I'm doing?" Ron replied, nudging the gaff's hook into the seam between drum and body, prodding at rust until the hatch popped free. The washing machine was a front loader, spilling its contents back into the sea. The water was black, disgorging small bones, likely the remains of whatever fish hadn't been able to find an exit.

Ron squinted into the murk, the innards of the machine seemingly coated with mud. Beneath the amorphous sediment, a hand passed through the mess, fingers curled back on themselves.

"What the hell?" Ron heard from over his shoulder. "That's not..."

"I think it is," Ron replied, not knowing whether he should drag the washing machine to the deck or leave it dangling over the water forever, not wanting to know what lay beneath the rest of the muck.

***

"Judging by the small amount of barnacles, it couldn't have been down there long," Kieron said as the three men watched a group of police officers struggle to ratchet the washing machine to a flatbed truck. They leaned against Jeremy's Ford, attempting to regain their equilibrium, having already given their statements. Ron hadn't thought of that. Usually the junk they recovered was coated in mollusks, seaweed thick as a blanket draped over their surfaces.

"Did you see what was drawn on the side?" Ron asked.

"No, I was a bit preoccupied," Jeremy replied. "Why?"

Ron paused, looking to Kieron for an answer.

"It looked like some weird crucified sea creature," Ron said. "Get a picture of it."

Ron lacked a smartphone. He disliked technology, worried about cancer. He hated the thought of devices pressed against his body. He'd read articles on the subject, blamed their invisible fingers for his wife's brain cancer. Mel would have been gone four years that October.

"Yeah, one second," Kieron said, jogging over to the flatbed. He reached an arm up, focused with a fingertip, and snapped a shot. One of the cops waved him off. *What should they care?* Ron wondered. A group of journalists from the *Cape Cod Times* had done the same thing an hour ago.

"Can you email it to me?" Ron asked.

"You email, but you don't text?" Jeremy asked.

"Yup. I'll open it at the library," Ron said, touching on a local joke. Ron spent more hours at the Wellfleet Public Library than anyone else in town. It was his second home. He loved the local history section, all those nonfiction texts on the rise and fall of fisheries along the coast, endless information on aquaculture and estuary rehabilitation.

"Sure. You need a ride?" Kieron asked.

"Thanks, but I'm set. My son's going to pick me up any minute."

"I'm going to say we're probably on hold for next week, right?" Jeremy asked. "Can't imagine it's a good idea to get back at it after something like this."

"I think that would be respectful," Ron said. "Poor kid."

Beneath the mud, there had been an arm, a head, a torso. The skin was bleached white, salt-worn and soft. The machine wasn't large enough to fit anymore. For a second, Ron's heart peaked. The man resembled his son. Clean shaven, messy hair, eyes close together, a solid chin. But the resemblance faded. He'd spoken to Richard earlier that morning. There was no way he could have ended up at the bottom of the bay so quick. Ron felt disgusted in his relief.

The body was still a man, even if the man wasn't blood.

***

The inside of Richard's car smelled of vanilla, the scent drifting from incense sticks wedged into the air vents. A wrap of dried flowers hung from the rearview mirror. Marsh grass and carved inlets passed by, small cottages leaning out toward the water. A white ibis darted through the shallows, stork-like. The car's shocks were old, every bump in the road coursing up Ron's seat, irritating the weak discs in his lower back.

"Was he the first?" Richard asked.

"Who?" Ron replied.

"The guy in the washer. Was that the first body you've found?"

"Of course. Are you kidding me? Why would there be more?"

"Just curious. People say weird stuff about the bay sometimes. At the bar, you know."

Richard worked at a small tavern at the end of Main Street called The Well. They sold cheap beer. Every surface was rustic varnished wood. Local folk bands played on Friday nights, one of the only entertainment options in the offseason. It paid the bills. Richard was banking on a career as a photographer, pulling wedding gigs through the busy season, but he was still trying to get his career off the ground. He took drone photos of beaches and lighthouses, selling them for cheap, mass-producing prints to hang in galleries along 6A. The money wasn't consistent, hence the nights spent at the bar. If people weren't buying art, they were still buying alcohol.

"Care to shine some light on that?"

"I don't know if I can. I'm sure it's just gossip, something the old guys make up when they're bored."

"You never know. It's surprising how many people go missing around here. Remember that guy from the movie shoot?"

"I doubt it's him," Richard replied.

Last summer, photos flickered across news channels, profiles of an extra who'd wandered off set and never came back. A girl he'd been staying with said he never collected his belongings, said they'd planned to stay together the rest of the summer. News channels looped her teary-eyed image more than the photo of the missing. Cops eventually said he was a drifter, moved on to the next town, the next party, having bled the local scene dry. It wasn't unheard of. Men screwed women on promises every day, shrugging off responsibility whenever a new scent came along.

"The movie was terrible. Not surprising he'd bail mid-shoot," Richard said.

Looking at his son, Ron hated how much he resembled the man in the machine. People weren't meant to die so young. It was trending. The number of overdoses and telephone pole collisions had skyrocketed. The suicide rate wasn't great either. Ron knew it wasn't easy to live on the peninsula. Rent was high. Housing was nearly impossible to find. Jobs were non-existent. But that wasn't a reason to blot out the rest of your days with a needle. He was glad his son found art. Some reason to live beyond balancing checkbooks and planning retirement.

***

Ron waited until the next morning to walk to the library, his nerves too keyed up to stare at a computer screen. He and his son lived in a single-story ranch a few streets over from Main Street. It needed a new roof and the siding was tinted green from moss blooms. His old quahogging skiff sat on a trailer in the driveway with no plans of seeing the water again. He told Richard he'd sell it when he needed to buy a new camera. Two raised garden beds stood on either side of their walkway, pepper and tomato seedlings beginning to unfurl their leaves. Ron only owned a postage stamp worth of acreage, but he made do. Green beans crawled up fence posts. A mulberry tree dropped purple berries into the clover below.

Ron didn't lock the door before leaving. He never did.

He trusted his neighbors, even if they were a bit aloof most days.

***

Gabrielle, the librarian behind the desk, waved as Ron pushed through the front doors. Her curly brown hair was held back by a blue bandana, her nose-ring dark against her pale skin.

"She's all ready for you," Gabrielle said, looking over at the computer Ron typically occupied.

"I've got to keep her waiting," Ron replied.

A bank of skylights let in slants of sun, illuminating a twisting tree potted next to a beam and several upended umbrellas dangling from light fixtures. The green carpets had been worn down from the heels of a thousand patrons. The scent of coffee seeped from the kitchen by the children's section. The library had once been a candle factory. It sprawled, high-ceilinged, row upon row of books stretching in every direction.

"I'm sure she won't mind," Gabrielle said. "Do you need help with anything?"

"Actually, have you got a moment?" Ron asked.

"My life is nothing but moments. What's on your mind?"

"Do you remember that guy who went missing last year? The actor?"

"Yeah. I read about it in the paper. I don't get cable, so, not much beyond that."

"They never found him, right?"

"Not to my knowledge."

"Did it strike you as weird?"

"Not particularly. Something like this happens every few years. With our population always in flux, people slip through the cracks."

"Any particulars?"

She paused.

"Well, there was that other actor who was here for the Tennessee Williams Festival. They had to cancel *Cat on a Hot Tin Roof* when he didn't show up opening night."

"Have anything on that?"

"If you feel like spending some quality time with the microfilm reader, I can definitely get you something," Gabrielle said.

***

The reel sped through twin dials, passing beneath a sheet of glass, reflected large on the screen above. Dates blurred. Ron halted the reels on a front page spread, the image of the missing actor juxtaposed by a shot of an animatronic shark. The man was twenty-three-year-old Michael Lenum. Ron scanned the following issues, tracking the story until its cold case conclusion.

Gabrielle left him with a second reel, dated three years prior. Ron found the pertinent covers, each depicting a thin man in his mid-twenties, a similar look as Michael, light hair, clear skin, gangly. He'd missed opening night. Wouldn't answer his phone. He'd been renting a room at a local hotel by himself. His mother and father hadn't spoken to him in years. They said as much in a phone interview. He was gay and they didn't approve of his lifestyle, citing religious reasons. Ron's stomach soured, disgusted by the paternal abandonment and bigotry. People were always disappointing him.

"And that's it?" Ron asked Gabrielle, who had been reading over his shoulder. The article ended the same way as the first.

"Unless you want to dig into every reel we've got. Until someone digitizes these, there's no other way to do a blind search."

"How long would that take?"

"Months, maybe years," Gabrielle replied.

Ron's eyes already stung from the quick blur of black words scrawling across the screen.

"In that case, you ever see anything like this?" Ron asked as he turned to a neighboring computer. He opened the email Kieron sent of the odd image on the side of the washing machine. "I feel like I've seen it before somewhere. Can't place it though."

Gabrielle took the mouse from the older man, zooming in.

"I've never seen a fish like that. Are those arms?"

"Maybe. I'm not sure. But the design. You recognize it?"

Gabrielle shook her head. "It looks old. If it's going to be anywhere, I'd check the local history section. I can take a look if you want?"

"No. It's fine. I'll see what I come up with," Ron replied.

***

Mel was an eighth-generation Cape Codder. She had liked to joke that she imported Ron to avoid kissing-cousin complications. Which, in truth, was a real concern. She told him a story of how she accidentally dated her second cousin for six weeks in high school, until they showed up at a family reunion...separately. Mel's roots were the reason locals were kind to him. He'd seen their hostility toward "washashores," a name given to those who came from the mainland. People joked about his own washashoredness, but he'd believed it to be good natured, even if he was self-conscious about his less aquatic upbringing.

Her picture was wedged into the edge of his bedroom mirror, long blonde hair disappearing out of the shot. She and Richard looked similar, eyes close together, deeply tanned.

In the next room, Richard was getting dressed for his shift at The Well, black from shoe to shirt.

Ron worried about his son. The money wasn't coming in as they'd hoped. Photography gigs were scarce. He didn't have the cameras or crew to do big weddings. Smaller ones were mostly friends paying small fees, pro bono jobs that came from the goodness of his heart.

"Are you guys going to look into it?" Ron asked, his landline telephone pressed to his ear.

"I'll have someone check. It sounds like a stretch though," the emergency operator said. Ron had dialed 911, relaying the connection Gabrielle spun into focus.

"I mean, the two men looked similar. They were both on the outside of things. Who knows how many washing machines might be down there."

"Just because they're cold cases doesn't mean they're linked."

"If you say so."

"We'll get a boat out sometime tomorrow."

Ron knew that wouldn't happen.

In the next room, Richard dropped something, following the clatter with a string of swears. It was probably his cologne. Richard was often frustrated before his shifts, never enjoying confrontation with drunks that inevitably arrived at the end of the night.

Why are we still here? Ron wondered, replacing the phone on its wall mount. He didn't have any close friends to speak of. Their house was worth an outrageous amount thanks to the inflated real estate market. Neither had anything particular anchoring them to the Cape any longer, despite Richard's insistence they stay. Richard could get work at a bar somewhere else, somewhere the cost of living wasn't so high. It was a question he found himself turning over. Beyond the library and the bay clean-up, what did he actually look forward to?

***

A week went by and Ron hadn't heard back from the police. The newspapers ran the articles he knew they would. *Body found in the Bay. John Doe.* No mention of the movie, no connection to the other actor or description of the odd symbol.

"You think they're being lazy?" Ron asked Richard as they weeded the garden beds.

"I don't know. I doubt they're going to jump on things based on a few theories," Richard replied, pulling up a strand of inkberry.

"But what if the theories have weight?"

"Do they really though? It's just two bodies."

"There might be more."

Ron bent by the potato patch, heaping more soil around the budding green stems. Ron didn't know how to explain why his mind had hung up on the bodies, how to explain he'd imagined his son in those waters, frozen beneath the waves.

"You think the guys at the bar might have a story or two?" Ron asked, digging his trowel into the dirt.

"I'm not asking them that," Richard replied.

"Then maybe I'll come down and ask."

"Come on, Dad, drop it. Nothing's going to bring that kid back, and this is only going to stress you out. You know your blood pressure isn't what it should be."

"I'll be fine," Ron replied.

He hadn't been able to shake the image of the young man sprawling out of the muck, the way his body had been shorn in half. He couldn't imagine telling another parent what he found, of breaking it to the mother and father.

People did such terrible things to one another.

***

The Well was dimly lit. Candles flickered on the heavily lacquered tables. The weekly folk band was breaking down their set, stuffing fiddles and banjos into velvet-lined cases. The din of voices spilled out into the night air as Ron opened the front door, greeted only by the smell of wood smoke from the unlit fire.

He made his way to the bar, where Richard stood with his back to the door, retrieving a bottle of whiskey. Ron pulled out a seat next to a group of older men, most wearing sweatshirts with the logo of the local fishing supply company across the shoulders.

"Can I get a beer?" Ron asked.

He rarely drank, so the words sounded wrong. The entire town knew. Several of the gathered men cocked their heads at the odd request.

Richard turned and shook his head.

He grabbed the lightest beer they carried, popped the cap, and handed it to his father.

"I thought you were going to drop it," he said.

"Just wanted to do a little fact-checking before I let it die," Ron replied.

"Whatever," Richard said, turning to another patron.

Ron sipped his beer and listened to the conversation going on around him. Mostly talk about sports teams he didn't follow and some upcoming catch restriction the government was levying. After a while, he leaned over, elbow on the counter, and inserted himself into their conversation.

"You guys see that bit about the washing machine on the news? Real sad about that kid," he said.

"Yeah, real sad," one of the men replied. "There are some real sickos out there."

"Haven't heard of something like that happening in ages. Not since that Tony Costa shit back in the sixties," another replied.

"But he wasn't dropping the bodies in the bay. Just his garden," Ron said. Everyone had read the book on the string of murders the man had committed, how he used the bodies for compost in his vegetable garden. "Ever hear of anything like this happening, with the water?"

The group of men looked among themselves, some peering into their beers, others out the back window, toward the marsh and the cattails waving in the darkness. Ron could feel his son's eyes, feel his mental nudging toward the door.

"Did any of you see that mark on the side of the washer? That in itself's real strange," Ron said.

"People used to carve it on their boats," a bearded man said from his seat by the window. "My father said it brought luck."

"Really?" Ron asked.

"Yeah. It's one of those holdovers from the old days. Superstitious stuff. People stopped carving it once they made better fish finders and radar. Don't need to pray when you've got technology," the man said.

"I've never read anything about it," Ron replied.

"It's a small thing. I don't think people really liked talking about it outside the community. It's a little embarrassing when you think about it," the older man said.

The group nodded agreement.

"Someone's probably just praying for the cod to come back like the rest of us," another man said.

Despite the name Cape Cod, cod were a rarity in their waters. They'd been overfished. Rising water temperatures forced the remaining schools farther out to sea. Ron had heard the usual gripe a thousand times. It was almost a non-response at that point.

"Anyone know anything..." Ron began before Richard's hand fell on his own.

"Let's stay away from the dark stuff tonight, Dad. You want another drink or are you all set?"

"I'm fine," Ron replied, rising from his stool, waving a casual goodbye to the other men.

"Don't think too much about it," the bearded man said as Ron walked toward the entrance. "Those old ways are dead."

***

Three weeks later, Ron, Kieron, and Jeremy were back on the water, trolling for debris. It was overcast. Few other boats were out. They'd already hauled in a barnacle-stuck outboard and a full rigging of lobster pots. Each discovery earned another line in the notebook, another statistic to feed back to conservation committees.

Each time the grappling hook dropped from sight, Ron's stomach dropped with it. He told himself there was no chance they'd dredge up another horror, but his fear was getting the better of him. He'd never felt seasick before, but his stomach swam in uneasy acidic loops, threatening to climb his throat.

"You going to be okay?" Kieron asked from where he stood by the winch.

Ron leaned against the side of the boat, staring down at the water, at the green-blue blackness of it. There was so much below he couldn't see, so much just beneath the surface.

"That washer's just..." Ron replied, straightening, trying to amend his posture.

"No one feels good after seeing a thing like that," Kieron said.

"Poor kid," Ron replied.

"No one would argue with you there," Kieron said, less earnestly than Ron had expected.

"Neither of you two knew him, did you? Didn't go to high school with him? Or play basketball or something?"

"I never saw him before," Jeremy replied from the front of the boat. "He looked like he would have been a bit younger than either of us. If he was a local kid, I'm sure someone would have claimed the body, or a missing person report would have kicked back a result."

"Probably some out-of-towner. Maybe one of those summer kids who party up in P-Town," Kieron added.

"That doesn't make it better," Ron said, eyes back on the water.

"At least it wasn't some local kid. There aren't many around these days, with everyone moving off Cape."

"No one would argue with you there," Ron replied as a shiver swept through the grappling line. It went taut, the winch's motor cutting through their conversation as Kieron began to reel in the line. It had hung up on something below. Ron retrieved the gaff from where he'd tucked it against the gunnel, ready to pull in whatever dangled from the end of the hook.

***

The library was empty, the overhead lights flickering out. It was nearly closing. Gabrielle paused by the computer where Ron sat, digitized issues of the *Cape Cod Times* shifting before him. She cradled a large flaking book in her arms, the leather binding mildewed from water damage. There was a red stamp over the library's barcode, the word WITHDRAWN inked in place.

"Is this the one you were talking about?" Gabrielle asked.

"Yeah," Ron replied. "I haven't seen it on the shelf in a while."

"You're lucky. It was in our recycling pile," she said, laying the book on a nearby desk.

Ron peeled back the cover and scanned through, stopping on a page with four columns of writing. On the far side was a grainy black and white photo of three men with what looked like a pirate chest between them.

"What's this? I've never seen it circulating," Gabrielle said.

"An old family scrapbook someone must have donated. It's got stuff in it dating back to the 1800s," Ron replied.

"And this article's about missing men?" Gabrielle asked.

"Not sure. I just remembered the picture from a while ago and wanted to take another look."

"Good. I'm glad you're making progress. Take your time with it. I've got to start shutting things down around here," Gabrielle replied before moving off into the stacks.

Ron leaned down, bringing his face near the aged paper. The glued-in strips of newsprint curled at the edges. There were the three smiling men, the boat, the sea in the background. They each held a handle of a large chest. On its side was carved a symbol similar to the one etched onto the washing machine, the odd fish, the crucifix.

He knew he'd seen it before.

The article was about old fishing traditions. Men filled chests with meat or shellfish or scraps from their hauls to throw back into the sea. It was supposed to ensure a good fishing season. To appease waterlogged gods and keep them from eating the rest of the year's catch. The article was originally published on August 7th of 1894.

The present date was August 6th.

Seasickness returned, the floor rocking beneath Ron's feet.

After her rounds, Gabrielle told Ron she would make photocopies for him, but her words barely reached his ear. His mind was elsewhere, paddling through a million ancient oceans, the murky bottom studded with washing machines, cemetery-like, stretching out of sight.

***

"What do you mean he didn't show up for work?" Ron asked The Well's manager, who stood behind the bar. The same group of men as before hovered by the windows, falling silent as Ron spoke.

"He was supposed to be in three hours ago. Figured he must have been sick. There's a stomach bug going around," the manager replied.

"He left the house on time. There's no reason he shouldn't be here," Ron said, sweat seeping from his pores, face reddening. He'd had a bad feeling since Gabrielle found the book and had begun doubting the people around him, borderline paranoia engulfing his thoughts.

"I'm sure he's out messing around with friends," the manager said.

"He would have told me first. We don't keep secrets like that."

"Richard's what, twenty-three? He's got to hide something sometimes," the manager said.

"It's not like that," Ron replied.

"I'd put money on it. He's out with some buddies, smoking weed, drinking. Just take it easy and go home. He'll show up."

There was a snicker from the huddle of men. "I'd put my money on something a little damper," someone muttered.

"What did you say?" Ron asked, turning on the group.

"You still got the dinghy, don't you?" the bearded man from weeks before asked.

"Yeah, why?"

"You might want to bring it down to the docks is all I'm saying."

"What do you..." Ron trailed off, shaking his head, long hair flailing across his face. No one was going to give him a straight answer. His mind clawed to worse places. The old guys knew something. They looked just like the men in the photo, their cracked smiles, the joke of meat hurried into the waves. They'd never really accepted Ron, he knew that, especially not since Mel died. They'd never considered him, or his son, one of their own. The thought sped Ron out the door, kicking up shells from the white-flecked parking lot.

***

The bay stretched before him. Ron left his truck on the launch ramp, e-brake hiked, keys in the ignition. If someone needed to move it, they could do it themselves. Ron couldn't wait. The endless void of stars leered down, singular eyes casting doubt he'd make it.

The entire fishing fleet bobbed on their moorings or by the docks. It was too late for anyone to be out. Ron sat on the dinghy's stern bench, the outboard's tiller in hand, speeding the small craft between lumbering charter boats and trollers. A distance out, there was a single prick of electric light blotting the sea. He aimed the bow at the illumination, the boat's keel cutting through waves rising around him. Flecks of salt spray split from the sea and stung his eyes. The wind whispered horrible things.

The dinghy wasn't going fast enough. The motor was a low-RPM model. It didn't have nearly as much kick as Ron remembered. Every nightmare scenario bled before his eyes: Richard dismembered, entrails drifting from his chest, a horde of old drunks shoving him into a washing machine, casting it off their boat. He could see his son's face staring up from beneath the waves, the scream stretching his lips.

The light grew closer, illuminating the faint outline of the boat it was mounted to. The boat became more familiar as he neared. He'd spent hours on its deck, reeling in rusted metal and trash. It was Kieron's boat. There was no doubting its looming silhouette.

Three shadowed figures stood on deck, surrounding a barrel, dipping in and out of sight as they bent toward the deck, retrieving things Ron couldn't see.

He slowed when he was fifty feet off.

The men on board stopped, staring over the side, tracking Ron's approach. As he grew near, he could see Kieron and Jeremy, their shirts tinted crimson, blood slicking down their wrists. Both looked confused, as if they couldn't place the man in the smaller craft.

"Ron, what the hell are you doing out here?" Jeremy asked, wiping his palms on his waders.

"What the hell am I doing?" Ron asked. "What the hell did you do to my son?"

As Ron spoke, he nudged the dinghy's bow against the fishing boat, looping a line around the rail as quick as he could.

"Hey, he came out here on his own," Kieron replied.

"What did you..." Ron began to say before the third shadow stepped into the light. Richard wore the same waders as the other two men, blood slick against the rubber, his forearms drenched in it. At their feet lay plastic containers of chum, odd cuts of meat and viscera floating in the troughs. By the transom stood a wooden barrel that looked like it belonged in an antique store, not on the sea. The symbol he'd seen carved into the washing machine adorned the side.

"Just head back in," Richard said. "I'll be home in a few hours. We've got to finish."

A string of nonsensical syllables drifted from Ron's lips, his confusions and fears pressing out against his skin, his throat swelling beneath their rising dread. He'd imagined his son, torn and tattered, in need of rescue. The joy he should have felt at his appearance was washed away with a new feeling of displacement, of fractured reality.

"What are you doing?" he managed.

"Someone has to feed them," Richard replied. "Mom said it was something I had to do when she was gone. It's always been this way."

"If they're hungry, they eat the fish," Kieron added.

"It's only logical," Jeremy said.

"Your mother never..." Ron stammered.

"Dad, just head back to the docks. You wouldn't understand. Our family's always done this," Richard replied.

"But the kid in the..."

"Let's not get into that," Kieron said.

"We thought they dropped that one farther out," Jeremy added.

"You were never meant to drag him up," Richard said.

Their words weren't melding, weren't forming logical patterns. Richard couldn't have known about the man in the machine, couldn't have sent him to the bottom. There wasn't anything else in the bay, nothing to eat the fish besides sharks and seals.

Ron's hand left the steel railing wrapping the boat's deck. The dinghy rocked beneath him as he stumbled to the bench, pulling the engine's rip cord. The burble of churned water and the cough of gasoline smoke fogged his vision. Peering up through the haze, he could barely make out his son's silhouette. Even in the failing light, he could still see the resemblance between mother and son. The narrow faces, the close eyes, that pull to their lips. Richard had never resembled him, their shared features nonexistent. Growing up, Ron waited for some glimmer of alignment to show, but their beings never overlapped.

In that moment, he understood why.

Pushing off from the larger boat, Ron throttled up, guiding the dinghy away. He pointed the bow north. The ocean reflected the sky, a million burning eyes leering down, their twins gazing up from below, unblinking, fixed in time.

From over his shoulder, he heard his son call out, "You're going the wrong way."

The wind swallowed whatever came next.

GREEN THOUGHT

The previous summer, Ralph and Chris had sworn to run together every morning in hopes of losing their baby fat. It was their freshman year of high school. Stories of eternal virginity and ostracism blurred their perceptions. They were anxious about transitioning from a small Catholic middle school to a large regional high school.

The plan had worked for two weeks before Ralph took up with a girl from a different neighborhood, abandoning Chris to his trails and desired weight-loss goals. But the romance flared out in months, months Ralph swore he regretted, apologizing for the injury it caused their friendship, the distance he'd placed between them.

"Hey, love's weird. I get it," Chris said, pushing his hair out of his face as they sat on the front steps of their school. "Just don't do it again, okay?"

"I'm not planning on it. Unless the next one's way hotter, or plays bass or something," Ralph replied.

Chris punched him in the arm. Ralph flinched, but only slightly. Ralph was taller than Chris, tan from the summer sun, hair shaved short. Chris was more compact, narrow-jawed, plastic-framed glasses correcting astigmatism. They wore t-shirts with the names of punk bands written across the chest, Dickies work shorts, and skateboard shoes.

"Next summer will be different," Chris promised, recalling the three months he had spent alone, the dark places his mind had wandered. Chris had no other friends. When Ralph wasn't around, he felt bisected, half-made, a phantom limb grasping with fingers no longer attached. They'd been together since first grade. No family member could boast the closeness he felt with Ralph. "We're going to get those runs in and make the cross-country team."

"Probably have to grow those legs a little longer then. I'll have my dad build us one of those stretching racks. The medieval ones."

"How about no," Chris replied, smiling. "I appreciate the creativity though."

2.

The next summer, after the first month of their running regimen, Chris and Ralph grew bored of their usual bike-path laps, the circuitous route around the dog park. They decided to take to the woods, carve paths through the overgrown forests. Chris's house abutted acre upon acre of undeveloped land. They traced deer paths between oaks and cedars, dipping beneath vines of bittersweet snaking between trees. When the woods grew thick, they'd change direction, veering around kettle ponds and fallow bogs.

Chris carried a compass. Due south was Route 139. There was no way to truly get lost.

"You ever worry we'll step into a coyote den?" Chris asked Ralph, trailing at his heels, the summer heat oppressive.

"They're nocturnal. They'd be asleep."

"But they'd wake up."

"Are you particularly quick in the morning?"

"Not really."

"They're probably the same. We'd be fine."

A thorny vine caught Chris in the shins, mid-step, sinking deep. He swore and stopped, gently easing the barb from his raw flesh. Sweat dripped down his face, trickling out of his hair. Ralph stopped a distance ahead, calling back to see if he was all right.

"Yeah, I'll be fine," Chris replied, shaking off the sting. He looked up from the tangle of vines, noticing a narrow corridor between a wall of evergreens. "Care for a change of direction?" he asked.

"Hell yeah," Ralph said. They'd been heading north for twenty minutes, the scenery uniform and forgettable.

The two slowed, pushing low branches from their path. The scent of pine overcame the humid breath of mulching leaves. Their sprint slackened to a jog. The press of trees was claustrophobic, pine needles gritty between their teeth.

When they came out on the other side of the tree-bound wall, the forest thinned. A huddle of moss-covered chimneys stood in an empty field, their cottage counterparts eaten away by time. Chris counted ten in all, some in better shape than others. Cracked pediments, slouching spines, trees growing between the mortar.

Without breaking stride, Ralph ran up to the first chimney, placing his hand on the weathered brick, looking out across the overgrown field.

"Your parents ever mention anything about this?" he asked, wiping sweat from his forehead.

"I doubt my parents ever actually walk in the woods," Chris replied. "They say it's where dark things end up happening. Real puritanical."

Earlier that year, Chris had refused to continue attending Mass with his parents. It had been a battle waged over several months. Groundings and innumerable repercussions followed. Disciplinary action eventually faded to passive-aggressive remarks about the state of his soul. His parents had given up.

Chris couldn't sit through the homilies, couldn't believe the creationist teachings of his earlier academic life. The break truly came when his biology teacher, Ms. Reilly, asked how to identify the sex of a human skeleton. He answered by the number of ribs, Adam having sacrificed one to create Eve. The laughter in the class still stung.

"Well, at least they keep life interesting," Ralph replied, walking to the next chimney, parting tall grass and clusters of holly saplings. Chris didn't like the feel of the place. Seeing the chimneys separated from the buildings made him think of abandonment. He'd never understood the idea of leaving a house to rot. The number of homeless people he'd seen lining Main Street in Hyannis made a case against any rational argument.

The small village was ringed with trees. No real road cut into the enclave. Chris felt hemmed in, as if something watched from the tree line.

"What do you think they were growing?" Ralph asked, kneeling by a patch of rough earth, a garden plot likely barren for centuries.

"Corn and squash. That's what they always grew around here. Potatoes maybe. I don't know," Chris replied, skirting the fallow field, attention drawn to a flare of color at the base of a distant chimney. It was a wreath of wildflowers, stems twined together, bloodroot and toadflax, lupine and chicory. Unlike the rest of the abandoned village, the garland was fresh, the clippings no more than a day severed. Chris picked up the ornament and breathed in the floral scent, the sweet aroma flourishing in his sinuses.

"Well, that's out of place," Ralph said, taking the wreath and inhaling deeply.

"Considering we're in the middle of nowhere," Chris replied, knowing they were at least a mile inland from the nearest road. "Yeah, it's super weird."

"Leave it."

"I wasn't planning on taking the thing home."

"Good. Your parents might be right about the whole dark woods thing. All we need now is to see a black goat wandering through the field and we'd have all the makings for a good found footage flick."

"*Blair Witch* was terrifying," Chris added, taking the wreath and dropping it back onto the brick hearth. "I'd prefer to avoid being an extra in the reboot."

3.

On the way to church the following Sunday, Chris's parents dropped him off at the library. A snarky comment about wasted time followed him from the car. Ralph met him out front. The renovated, white-fronted colonial was within walking distance of his house, the path shaded by horse chestnuts and aged birch. The library was open only a few hours. A skeleton crew staffed the front desk. They'd have to make the most of their time.

Beforehand, they'd googled every combination of words that might lead to some understanding of the chimneys. Abandoned village. Harwich, MA. Forgotten towns of Cape Cod. Chimneys abandoned in the woods. Every attempt brought disconnected results. None shone light on their recent running route. They'd trekked through the village three times since, on each iteration winding between the brick outcroppings, noting the wreath's gradual wilt.

Pushing through the front doors, they were confronted by the portrait of Mr. Brooks, the library's namesake, done in dark oils.

"That guy would have definitely known the answer," Ralph said, passing by his gaze.

"Or at least pointed us toward the right book," Chris replied.

The library was all high ceilings and expansive rows of books, mismatched plush chairs and graying carpet. A circular display hunkered in the foyer, exhibiting the latest releases and summer reading suggestions. Natural light bled through high windows. One of the librarians directed the two upstairs, to the reference section and computers designated for research.

After another hour of fruitless internet reconnaissance, they abandoned the computers and approached the reference librarian, seated behind a desk lined with encyclopedic texts that looked as if they hadn't been opened in years. The bearded man's nametag read *JACK*.

Chris didn't know exactly how to phrase his question. He didn't want it to seem like they were sneaking around somewhere they shouldn't, or like they were trying to play a practical joke on the man. He always feared such things would make their way back to his parents and they'd forbid him from hanging around Ralph anymore.

As Chris hesitated, Ralph filled the silence. "Do you know anything about a small village out in the woods about four miles that way?" he asked, doing his best to point in the right direction.

"Are we talking Harwich, Chatham, or Brewster?" the man asked.

"Harwich. At least we get to it through Harwich. It might be in Brewster if I really think about it," Chris answered.

"Well, you'll have to narrow it down. There were a few villages that didn't make it through the years out that way," Jack said, nodding.

"It would have been somewhere a mile or so north of Route 139. Does that help?" Chris asked.

"Actually, it does," Jack replied, rising from his desk and walking into a row of shelves cordoned off from the public with a velvet rope.

"That's where they hide the *Necronomicon*," Ralph whispered. They'd snuck in a showing of *Evil Dead* on their last sleepover. Chris's parents refused to let him watch R-rated movies, but Ralph's didn't care. They thought Chris was too sheltered. A little demon possession wouldn't hurt.

Jack returned with a thin book bound in cracked leather. "We don't let people take this one out, and we usually don't let people take it out of sight. You two can read it over at that table," he said, pointing to the scarred wooden fixture next to a shelf of periodicals. "Chapter six. That one might make more sense for your purpose."

"Thanks," the two said in unison, carrying the book to the designated space.

There was no title, just a call number of 974.4 HAR. The early chapters detailed cranberry harvesting techniques, the founding of the first school within town limits, early interactions with the indigenous Wampanoag people, and brining methods using salt harvested from local inlets. The first page of chapter six showed what appeared to be a mask stitched together from dried leaves, the edges overlapping to obscure the wearer's eyes. The section was titled "Heretics of the Green Thought."

"Jesus, that's a terrible name," Ralph said.

"Really? Is it any better than Peoples Temple or Heaven's Gate? At least it's floral," Chris replied.

"Fair enough."

The next page showed a charcoal sketch of a rustic hamlet hemmed in by trees, large stretches of tilled soil neighboring each cabin. In the background, the stooped forms of peasants plucked something from the earth, but Chris couldn't tell what. The subsequent five pages detailed how the town existed outside the surrounding villages, growing its own food, avoiding Puritan churches nearby in favor of pagan approaches to spirituality.

The article said that most inhabitants had been pushed out of the church for their repudiation of strict scriptures. The town of Green Thought existed for almost thirty years before people from neighboring communities started going missing. A total of twelve men and women disappeared from Chatham, Brewster, and Harwich over a two-year stretch. A local vigilante group, members of the church and the loved ones of those lost, decided to search the village and interrogate the inhabitants. It took only two hours to force a confession out of a young man. Second thoughts about abandoning the church plagued his conscience.

The people of Green Thought needed fertilizer to appease their deity, an omniscient presence promising to restore the land to nature, all nonbelievers swallowed by vine and tendril. The crowd unearthed the bodies of two men in a nearby potato field and the body of a woman in an onion patch.

The book didn't detail the punishment for those who murdered their neighbors, but it wasn't hard for Chris to guess. They'd read *The Crucible* in English class. Salem was only a short drive north.

"How does no one talk about this?" Chris asked the reference librarian when they returned the book.

"People don't talk about a lot of things," the man replied. "How do you think people believe half of what they do? The answer to most things is out there, people just don't take the time to look."

"How did you know where to find the information?" Ralph asked.

"I wrote an article on it for the *Harwich Chronicle* a few years back. I freelance as a local historian. People love a buried cult story," Jack replied.

4.

The next week, they told themselves they'd stay away from Green Thought, but every path through the woods led back to the abandoned chimneys. Even when they swore they'd stick to the bike path, they ended up in the clearing. Chris would take out his compass and scratch his head at the way west had become east, how his directional inclinations fell apart before his eyes. After a time, he gave up fighting, allowing the village to draw them near despite the nucleus of fear blossoming in his chest.

Curiosity always won out.

Sometimes, after they entered the clearing, Ralph would ask if Chris had heard something, tilting his head toward the imagined sound. The words Ralph claimed to hear, the crooning insistence to sow seeds and harvest thistle, never resonated with Chris. It only made him worry about Ralph's senses, the sway the story held over his friend.

"It's the power of suggestion," Chris said as they ran the perimeter of the village.

"It was real close this time. Like the person was next to me," Ralph replied.

"We've literally watched nothing but horror movies for months. When I look into my back yard at night, I see deer skeletons by the shed. But they're not there. It's a flicker, confusion between screen and reality."

"Is that something your parents told you?"

He hadn't realized he'd regurgitated one of his mother's aphorisms, one of the reasons she'd been so strict with movie privileges.

"I guess it is," he replied before skidding to a stop, nearly twisting an ankle on a rotting log. Where the day before there had been a weed-choked plot of bramble, crabgrass, and mullein, there was now bare earth, freshly turned, raked lines dividing the space into even rows. Chris waited, ready for his vision to realign, carpeting the soil with tangled vines and greenery, but the verdant blanket never rolled into place. Someone had been digging in the garden, getting it ready.

"Still looking for that black goat," Ralph said, eyes wandering from the tilled garden to the tree line.

"Shut up," Chris replied. "No one's bringing a goat out here. This, though, this is bad. There's no reason someone would walk into the middle of the woods to do their gardening."

"There's a land shortage," Ralph replied. "Mom talks about it all the time. Her coworkers have a rough go finding rental property..."

"That's not what I'm talking about."

"I know, just trying to lighten the situation."

"Don't."

"It's fine. I'm sure next time we're out here, nothing will change...unless that voice is right. Like you said, no one's coming out here to grow cabbage."

5.

Over the course of two weeks, more and more of the tangled undergrowth around Green Thought was tilled and turned over, exposing rich brown soil. With each lap around the abandoned village, Chris's stomach gnawed inward, the fear of the book's citations haunting his mind. The bodies buried in the field, the harvest from neighboring communities. Wasn't his house one of the closest to the forest? Didn't his parents forget to lock the doors at night? Chris liked to think he was more mature than his years, but when such thoughts assailed him, he found himself crawling back to infancy, base fears clouding his vision.

He'd been raised on the Bible and all its supernatural logic. Resurrection. Angels. Whale digestion. How was a woodland deity any different from a vengeful God? The thought wouldn't leave Chris no matter how much he wanted it gone.

"That's a lot of effort to go through if you're not going to start planting," Ralph said.

"It's too late in the growing season. There's no way anything's going to come up," Chris replied.

"Unless they're burying something else. With the right fertilizer, who knows? It's like the voice said."

"There's no voice."

"You're probably not listening."

"I am, and there's nothing there."

"Don't be so sure of that," Ralph said, running toward the path leading away from Green Thought. Chris wanted to linger, to examine the soil further, but he didn't want to do it alone, and Ralph obviously wasn't into the idea of surveying the site.

6.

The bones appeared the next week, some whole, others powdery fragments poking through the soil, femurs ground short, clavicles yellowed with age. They seemed haphazard in their arrangement. No care had been taken to hide their presence from wandering eyes. Chris and Ralph stood over the empty plot, the only visible growth belonging to the undead osteology collection. The powdered bones lent a whitened appearance to the soil, mellowing the rich brown it had been before. Chris squatted, retrieving what might have been a minute bone from a human hand, or a leg bone from a squirrel. There was no saying which was which.

"So how are we feeling about the whole not believing thing?" Ralph asked, watching as Chris pushed the bone back into the soil after wiping it off on his shirt. He didn't want to leave fingerprints in case the authorities stumbled on the clearing.

"These bones are old. Whoever's doing this isn't out killing people to fertilize their crop," Chris replied.

"Maybe they haven't worked themselves up to it yet. This could be step one, easing into the deep end. Just because you don't want to believe it doesn't mean you're right."

"That's not it. We don't even know if these belong to humans."

"We don't know they don't. Regardless, this is sketchy. There's no reason to bury bones in a garden. This is straight out of that book."

A flock of sparrows dropped into the glade, some alighting in neighboring pines, others perching on the chimneys, peering down at where Chris and Ralph stood. A shiver passed through Chris's limbs. The birds focused on them, their tiny eyes moving from the bone-strewn plot to the teenage boys in their running shorts and band t-shirts. Chris felt vulnerable, laid bare. The birds chirped and squabbled before taking wing, leaving the friends to sort what lay before them.

Is that the voice Ralph had been hearing? Chris wondered. *The chattering of birds?* There was no way to mistake their chitters for actual sentences. He knew he was searching for grounding, something to explain the unraveling reality before him. Nothing was lining up. He couldn't find his footing.

"Believe what you want. I see a fully tilled field. The book said this was part of the buildup. We both know what their next step is. Either we're going to do something about this or we're not," Ralph said.

"How about we pretend we didn't see this and run the indoor track after school instead," Chris said.

"You know that isn't an option, no matter how much you wish it were. No one else is going to stop this."

Ralph had always been more inclined to action, less research, more bravado. He didn't like to wait or ask permission. Chris figured that was why the girl from last summer chose Ralph over him. They were attractive in similar ways since they'd lost weight, minus the height difference. Their interests and hobbies aligned. It was Ralph's confidence that made him more desirable.

Chris couldn't bring himself to argue. The dread of pushing Ralph away with disagreement rivaled any leaf-choked Armageddon he could imagine. But he was imagining a leaf-choked Armageddon, so there wasn't even that.

"So what do you want to do?" Chris asked.

7.

"Doesn't this seem a bit extreme?" Chris asked, holding the hand scythe Ralph unearthed from his father's potting shed. The man was a professional gardener and reserved an entire outbuilding for his soil and spare ceramics. Small seedlings wound pale roots through several grow trays, waiting to be ensconced in a more permanent home. The setting sun crept through the small windows positioned high in the walls, the scent of organic fertilizer acidic and sour.

"If you consider this person's beliefs, who knows? I wish you could hear what the voices... Well, I don't want a thousand tree branches tapping on my window tonight, asking me to come outside. If they're planting the bones, then they're serious," Ralph said, testing the weight of an axe against his palm.

"And you're going to be able to swing that into someone's skull?" Chris asked, gesturing to the axe.

"If it comes to that, yeah."

Chris had never been good with violence. On the screen it was one thing. In his personal life, not so much. He'd never been in a fistfight, never had his eye blackened over a gym class brawl. Ralph had been a scrapper since they were young. The scar from a dozen stitches traced his left forearm, a reminder of the kid who had tried to steal their skateboards in seventh grade. But Chris had his doubts. The violence Ralph had been capable of was minimal, never something with consequence. Murder was in another category.

"Is it the voices?" Chris asked.

Ralph shrugged. "This is the logical progression of things. These people are coming after our families. We're going after them. It balances out."

"And the cops?" Chris asked, his last holdout for resolution aired.

"You think they're going to believe us about some farm in the woods and a book with no title that exists only at the library? Even if we showed them the body, they'd say it was a hoax or some old deer carcass. No one believes stuff this far away from what they expect."

"I know," Chris replied.

Years of listening to punk anthems had made him suspicious of police involvement anyway. He just wanted to keep his hands free of blood and saw no other way to broach the subject.

"Don't worry. You'll be the backup. Maybe you won't even have to use that thing," Ralph said, clanging the axe head against the curved blade of the scythe. A ringing note sang through the small shed, trilling in Chris's ears. It reminded him of the sounds of shovels striking stones in preparation for the season's first sowing.

8.

They told their parents they were sleeping over at one another's houses. Their weekends were rarely spent any other way.

Before it got dark, Chris and Ralph tucked their blades beneath black hoodies, ducking into the forest a distance down the road from

Chris's driveway. They couldn't follow the path they usually took from his back yard. The lie wouldn't stick.

The setting sun sifted through pitch pines and oaks, staining the leaf-choked forest floor with emaciated shadows, the first hints of fall in the air. A flock of grackles chittered in overhead limbs, their calls reminiscent of unoiled door hinges, rusted and grating. The two moved quietly, not knowing when the second party would arrive. Surprise was the only way. Their pace was cautious, sidestepping brittle sticks and twigs cast off by old growth.

Chris tried to form a complaint, a reason to turn back, but the excuse wasn't forthcoming. He didn't want to disappoint. He was cautious with his words, the fear of a solitary existence plain before him. His stomach rose into his throat, pulsing with each step, nerves threatening to override conscious thought.

They weren't turning back.

At Green Thought's tree line, they paused, scanning the withered village for signs of life. The chimneys cast angular shadows across the unkempt greenery. The garden plot on the far side of the glade had receded farther, more bare earth peering through the underbrush, more bones speared up in ragged protrusions. Ralph gestured toward a chimney on the opposite side of the field. It was the closest to the trees and would provide the most cover.

"Stick to the trees until we get there," Ralph said, gesturing with the axe.

"Yeah, okay," Chris stuttered, the soft padding of moss giving way beneath his step.

When they were hidden by the blind of a holly tree, Ralph turned to Chris, whose hands were trembling.

"It's going to be fine. You've always wanted to be a hero, right?" Ralph asked.

"I mean, who doesn't?" Chris replied.

"Good. Someone's always got to be there to brain a zombie or exorcise a demon. Think of it like that. We're here to stop cultists from taking over our town, or something like that."

"I know, I know. It's just hard to imagine the next step."

"It is. But someone needs to be there before they get too far. When carnivorous plants crawl across your front porch, there's no hindsight. I'm not letting those things get my parents."

Ralph fell silent. The trees on the other side of the glade quivered and disgorged a man pushing a wheelbarrow. A leaf-stitched mask obscured his face. He whistled, high and off-key. The wheelbarrow seemed to give the man some difficulty, even though it only contained a minimal assortment of tools. Chris recognized the mask from the pages of the nameless book, the way the leaves wove together to cover the eyes and give the impression of a blank surface.

Chris prayed he wouldn't recognize the face it hid.

The scythe's handle was rough in his palm, the wood coarse and unfamiliar. The image of the blade slipping into the man's chest flourished with each blink of the eye, churning Chris's stomach, blood slicking Chris's fingers.

He turned, ready to run.

Ralph caught him.

"Just wait. It's not time yet."

Ralph had mistaken Chris's flight for an overzealous strike. He'd missed the desperation in Chris's eyes, the heave and shiver in his chest. He couldn't hear the chittering scream welling inside Chris.

"A few more minutes and we'll be set," Ralph said as Chris squatted, fleeting courage pulling him back to earth.

Then the man removed his mask.

Moonlight fell upon aged features. Overgrown eyebrows swam above a sea of wrinkles. His hair was brushed in a thin comb-over, eyes focused on the patch of upturned earth. Chris nearly dropped his scythe. The man looked like every lonely parishioner he'd seen hunched in a church pew, the priest's call for thoughts and prayers announcing a sickened spouse. He'd seen the man's countenance replicated a thousand times in those that were left behind. Those who'd lost the one thing guiding them to draw breath. Chris saw the worry and sadness engraved on the man's skin, the distance between the world he wanted to live in and the one he inhabited.

"We're not... " Chris began.

"That man wants your family dead, swarmed by flower petals until they choke. Don't bail on me," Ralph replied, clutching the axe to his chest.

"He's just a gardener. A lonely old man."

"A lonely old man that's wearing a cult mask. And the bones. You can't explain that away."

"What do you..."

"Even if he doesn't seem like he's trying to kill you, he is. Cause and effect. He wants to bury us all in his garden."

With the last words, the old man stopped unloading his wheelbarrow, looking up from the pile of rakes to where the two boys hid in the holly. His hand drifted to where the discarded mask lay, as if he hoped to hide beneath it.

"Who's there?" he called.

"Don't make me do this alone," Ralph said, stepping from cover, axe raised. Then he was running, full sprint, the weapon before him. Chris was running too, breaking from the undergrowth, following his only friend's footsteps, scythe catching the glint of moonlight as he trailed behind. The last thought left to him was of Ralph's body twisted and mangled beneath the roots of an ageless oak, life crushed from his limbs by swelling bark and heartwood. That was the world the old man had painted, the verdant monstrosity he had breathed into life.

The man was feet away.

The scythe no longer felt unfamiliar in Chris's hand.

THE MAN OF REEDS
AND SEAWEED

The Man of Reeds and Seaweed attempted to blend with the invasive phragmites growing beneath the bridge. His gangly arms draped into the water, bulbous head tucked between backward-jointed knees. The phragmites resembled cattails, something like an aquatic wheat field brushed by the current. His coloration was off. The vines and ferns sprouting from his body were a dull, burnt brown where they needed to be pale. He failed to adapt to new flora, sticking out like a colored illustration in a black and white world.

Fred hated pointing him out on his tours—camouflage was camouflage for a reason—but it was what the people wanted, what paid the bills at the bird sanctuary. They couldn't afford to lose donations with the most recent land grab under way. One hundred and fifty acres of brackish wetland would be on the market at the end of the month and their fundraising goals were abysmal.

"What does the marsh man eat?" a young boy asked from the back of the group, binoculars pressed to his eyes.

There were twelve people huddled close on the nature trail, all carrying bird-watching equipment. Some wore wide-brimmed hats. Others smelled of sunscreen. They'd passed a glossy informative plaque minutes before. All the basic biological information on Reeds, as he was affectionately known, was spelled out in simple terms. But the boy must have missed it or was too young to read about the species' thousands of years in the same marsh or their once prominent role as apex predators.

"A little meat. A little vegetation. He's omnivorous. Usually we see him catching fish, pulling reed grass from the riverbank," Fred replied.

"Why's he so skinny?" the boy asked.

"There aren't as many fish in the river as there once was and the phragmites pushed all the reed grass out. Phragmites just don't taste as good. Too much fiber."

The crowd laughed at Fred's joke even as the words soured in his throat. He hated making light of Reeds' predicament, but humor brought in more money than the dour reality of diminishing habitat. No one wanted to hear about apex predators reduced to skeletal remains, all the wolves and bears and cougars, their trail to the end nearly identical. Only the time and place varied.

"He's a protected species, right?" the boy's mother asked.

"Well, yes. Technically he's functionally extinct, but you never know," Fred said.

The boy lowered his binoculars.

"So he's going to..."

"Like I said, you never know," Fred replied.

***

"Did you see the trail cam footage?" Beth, Fred's supervisor, asked the next day as they punched their timecards. The central education building was two miles downstream from where they'd seen Reeds on the last tour. It was a modern, glass-walled structure composed of classrooms, office space, rehab tanks, and lecture halls.

"I didn't, why?" Fred asked. "Is he eating the turtles again?"

The turtles in question were diamondback terrapins, an endangered species with a glimmer of hope at a comeback.

"No, it's not that," she replied. "He was up here, walking around the building, knocking on windows, trying doorknobs."

"That doesn't sound like him."

"No, it doesn't, and it's a little concerning."

"Should we cancel the tours?

"Oh god no. We can't afford to lose the revenue."

Fred knew that. He had three tours scheduled for the day and a potential fourth if enough phone calls came in. With the neighboring land getting bought up, more and more people were taking their last chance to see Reeds. Word had gotten out that if the land was developed, there wasn't much chance for survival.

"But what if he..." Fred began.

"Keep your distance. They have binoculars for a reason," Beth replied.

***

A belted kingfisher peered into shallow water searching for minnows. A pair of white ibis panned about the reeds. An osprey nest sang with the squall of fledglings above the walking path. Fred pointed to each as they passed, noting identification details, behaviors common to the species. He prayed it would be mostly birds that morning, that Reeds was tucked away somewhere, maybe eating his first decent meal in months.

Two twenty-somethings at the back of the tour wore matching Reeds t-shirts, the marsh man's face done in tie-dye. He knew there wasn't much chance at avoiding the subject.

He'd spotted Reeds' tracks earlier, leading down to the muddy banks of the river, away from the education center. He hadn't pointed them out. It was important to avoid false hopes.

They didn't see Reeds every day. Sometimes he slept in his nest that they had never been able to locate. Sometimes he managed to find a stand of native plants he could actually blend with. Sometimes he was passed out asleep in the middle of a path. Fred never knew what they were going to get.

Fred didn't think of himself as fatherly, but maybe more of a concerned uncle, a godfather waiting for the phone call after an ill-fated plane crash. He loved the creature from a distance. Like he said the day before, Reeds was omnivorous.

For a while, he'd left food out, deli meat and watercress salads, until Beth caught him and said he had to stop. It was one of the tenants of conservation: not introducing another unsustainable means of survival. Fred wouldn't always be there to share a sandwich and some sushi, so it was better for Reeds to not get accustomed.

Since then, Fred had been thinking of other, less noticeable ways to help, but he'd been drawing a blank.

"Is that the marsh man?" one of the two t-shirt clad enthusiasts shouted, drawing Fred from daydreams.

He squinted, covering his eyes from the sun.

There was no doubting it. Reeds hunched by a small pool on the side of the river where the current was weak. A number of turtles swam around him, the silver scales of fish sparkling about his ankles. His own vegetation drifted into the water, casting shadows across the surface. Fred couldn't tell what he was eating, but Reeds had his hands by his mouth, the faint sound of chewing reaching them.

"Yup, that's the Man of Reeds and Seaweed. Now, if we're real quiet and keep our distance, we'll be able to observe him for a bit before we move on," Fred said.

"Move on?" one of the enthusiasts said. "Why don't we just camp out here all day? You're kidding yourself if you think any of us came for the birds."

An elderly man with a birding guide to North America in hand moved to correct them, but stopped mid-gesture, tucking his book into his backpack.

"Well, we can stay for a while, but not too long. We don't want to disturb him more than necessary," Fred said.

"Whatever you say, man," the twenty-something replied.

Reeds continued to eat with the fish surfacing around him, fighting the current's pull, nipping at scraps of food dropped into the water. It almost looked like Reeds was feeding them, his own open-borders aquarium. The group watched in silence, binoculars raised, some jotting lines in notebooks or doing quick sketches of the creature. Whispers circulated in pods. Some thrilled at the noises. Others were moved to tears.

Then someone gasped, "What's he eating?"

Fred hadn't focused on the meal itself, just the muscular figure hunched in the shallows. He brought his own binoculars up, training them on what Reeds held.

Fred gagged, bile climbing his throat.

It was a human arm, wrist to shoulder, pale and decayed.

"Is that a..." a young girl began to ask.

Her question was cut off by Reeds turning, black eyes narrowing in their direction, almost waving the arm in a twisted gesture of welcome. The little girl, and half of the group, screamed in unison before running down the path they'd just taken. Fred had to grab both the enthusiasts by the shoulders to force them to follow. They were too busy snapping photos, eyes wide, some dream fulfillment flashing before them.

Fred couldn't let them linger. He didn't know what Reeds would do, especially with his meal interrupted and a newly discovered food source.

"Run!" Fred yelled, pushing them toward the education center.

They tripped over themselves, stumbling up the path, casting glances over their shoulders in an attempt to see if the marsh man was going to follow, if he was still hungry.

***

"I'll write up the report," Beth said, sitting across from Fred in the break room, twin microwavable burritos steaming between them. "It's traumatizing enough having to see that, let alone write about it."

"Shouldn't we call someone? Like the police?" Fred asked.

"You know what they do to tigers in India when they start eating people, right?"

Fred nodded. He read about the shooting of the endangered big cats, the way quick concern morphed into violence in seconds.

"Yeah, but whose arm was it?" Fred asked, the beef and bean scent of the burrito turning his stomach.

"Who knows? Could have been something washed in from the sea. You never know these days, with ships going down and all the sharks along the coast. He probably just picked it out of the water."

"So you think he didn't kill someone for it?"

"No way. He's pretty peaceful. More of a scavenger than anything else, right?"

"I guess," Fred replied.

"Just bring the gun with you on your next tour. He's like a grizzly. Fire into the air and he'll run away."

"We're not canceling the other tours?"

"Nope. You'll be fine. Like I said, he's just a scavenger."

***

Fred didn't find Reeds on his third or fourth tour of the day. The marsh man had melted back into the marsh or returned to his nest to enjoy the rest of his meal in peace. The weight of the pocketed revolver was a terrible reminder of potential, a forked reality Fred wanted nothing to do with. Each of the tour groups lamented the lack of the main attraction, but they had seen a number of herons and a bald eagle, so a portion of the discontent was alleviated. Part of Fred would be glad when all there was to see would be birds, simple and nonthreatening. Part of him dreaded it.

***

"I can wait if you'd like," Fred told Beth as she sat in her office, computer screen laden with emails and Word documents.

"Naw, I'm backlogged. You'd be here all night," she replied with a smile. "I'm taking a half-day Friday, so don't feel bad."

"Are you sure?" Fred asked.

"One hundred percent. I'll grab some takeout and wine on the way home as a treat. It all balances out."

***

Albert, Fred's half-chihuahua, half-pitbull, greeted him at the door to his apartment. Fred was thankful Beth hadn't made him wait. Albert didn't have the best bladder control and it was almost feeding time.

The apartment was small: a bedroom, a kitchen, a bathroom. He'd tried to fill it with as many terrariums as he could, recreating habitats he saw throughout his day, or ones he glimpsed in nature documentaries. Fred wanted to understand the world around him, how he could help, where the pieces fit together. With Reeds, he'd felt like a failure for the past year, his tours never able to bring in enough money. The op-eds he wrote to local newspapers changed no one's mind. If the money wasn't there, the owners of the land weren't going to reconsider. The calendar hanging on his wall had a large red circle on the day of the land auction. Those few weeks between seemed too scant to count, an inevitability approaching too quick.

Albert licked at his hand, then sniffed at his food dish.

"Don't worry, I didn't forget," Fred said, retrieving the bag of kibble from the cabinet. "We all need to eat."

***

Fred was early for work the next morning.

The legs jutting from beneath the bushes that greeted him wore black heels.

Torn stockings disappeared into the undergrowth.

Fred traced a line of blood leading from the path between the education center and the parking lot. His heart quickened. A viscous lump pooled in his throat. He walked toward the shrubbery, leaning forward, before the crack and snap of branches tore his attention away. In the distance, a shape plowed through the forest. Fred's eyes shifted from the body to the front door, fight or flight flickering in his veins.

The body was still. There wasn't anything he could do, so he sprinted to the front door, hurrying with his keycard, palms sweaty as the nob finally turned. The air-conditioned breath of the center surrounded him, that filtered scent, the splash of rehab pools drifting from deep inside the building. In the distance, the crash of tree limbs grew louder. The entire building wasn't much more than one continuous window bisected by steel girders. It felt as if he were still in the woods, leaves pressing against his face.

Fred watched Reeds approach, indifferent to what lay in his path, tearing pine and oak limbs, uprooting small saplings. In moments, they were face to face, Reeds' large black eyes peering in at him, his face wrapped in algae and vines and the reeds for which he was named. His hollow mouth chewed the air, a nearly toothless cavern opening and closing.

Fred pulled his cellphone from his pocket. He dialed 911, but hesitated before pressing send. He knew what the cops and animal control officers would do if they showed up, the tigers flashing through his head. Fred didn't know if he'd blame them after seeing Beth's body in the bushes. She didn't deserve what happened, but pressing send meant the death of an entire species. He could blame the other factors leading to this moment, the lack of food, the lack of habitat, but the final nail would belong to him if he made the call.

Reeds ran a finger over the glass, breath fogging the pane, searching for an ingress to get to Fred. The smooth surface led to nothing, so the creature slammed his palm against the barricade. The glass shivered, barely holding. Something at the edge whined. The sound of a thin splinter ran through the surface.

Fractals spread, obscuring Reeds' mouth, his eyes, his grasping hands that kept slamming into the window.

Fred couldn't bring himself to press send as he ran into the interior of the building, assessing which door would be the thickest, which locks the sturdiest. Beth had told him he wasn't allowed to tamper with Reeds' diet. They weren't permitted to interfere. It was part of conservation.

Maybe the right door/lock combination would hold. Maybe Reeds would wander deeper into the building to feed from the turtle rehab tanks. Maybe he'd get bored and leave.

Regardless, Fred couldn't make the call.

Nature had to play itself out.

TO TEND A GROVE

1.

My crew took coffee breaks on the rusting golf carts parked beside the old clubhouse. Each vehicle was up on blocks, wheels stripped, waterproof upholstery giving way to moss and lichen and dry rot. My guys didn't mind. They'd eat breakfast sandwiches reclining beneath their hole-punched plastic roofs, waiting for the next truck of plant stock to be delivered. I passed them like I had every morning for a year and a half, offering a wave, but not stopping long enough to truly shoot the shit and get excited about the new trees we'd be adding to the landscape.

I always hated being the bearer of bad news.

I needed to get it over with quick.

The clubhouse itself was a step or two away from collapse. Lucas said he was going to have it torn down when the trees were planted and the trails lined, but for the moment, the structure was a reminder of 50's-era decay. The white-painted siding was tinted yellow from years of pollen and lack of pressure washing. The green and white window awnings luffed in the wind, torn to tatters from long neglect. The porch was missing boards, paint flaking like a particularly aggressive skin condition. I didn't know how long Lucas had been living in the old golf pro shop, but I had no idea how he put up with such disintegration day after day.

With all the money he threw into the arboretum, you'd think he'd spruce up a few things around his home. A fresh coat of paint. Swap out the rotting boards. Maybe hammer down the rusting nails that protruded from everything, catching coat sleeves and jacket hems with each step, but nope. He had only one thing on his mind.

I knocked on the glass door that led into Lucas's combination bedroom-living room-kitchen-office. The building had an open floor plan, which didn't lend itself to delineating one part of life from the next. At least the bathroom had its own separate door.

I knocked again.

No answer.

Probably hungover, I guessed as I leaned against the tinted window, shielding my eyes so I could see inside. The room, much like the rest of the building, was in disarray. A mattress rested at the room's center, layers of sheets balled up at the end, pillows thrown around the floor. The kitchen table, a few feet away from said mattress, was covered with sauce-stuck plates and beer bottles, a mix of plant-related paperwork lying beneath it all, invoices for another hundred shagbark hickories, two hundred black cherries.

A wad of clothing on the couch could have been a body, but could also have been a month without a trip to the laundromat.

I didn't know the actual answer, but it didn't seem like Lucas was in.

Plants appeared to be the only living things within. On every available surface stood some odd variety of tree or shrub, cyprus and pomegranate and filbert, all growing from ceramic pots, leaning into the sunlight drifting through skylights and outer windows. The man was obsessed. There had to be a hundred, the swirl of human chaos brushing up against their pots, odd socks and undergarments strewn in their branches.

I raised my fist to knock again, but something shifted by a leafy hibiscus. A black smear crept across the back corner of the room, long-limbed, thin beyond belief. I knew Lucas wasn't eating well, but I never figured he'd reached a state of emaciation, nor did I think he'd try to skip out on me when I came calling.

The silhouette stepped to the sliding door, yanked it open, and passed through. I swore and ran around the side of the building, my canvas overalls not the most athletically designed garment for the task.

He had no reason to run.

He paid his bills on time.

I wasn't there to collect debts.

I sprinted the opposite way from the golf carts, not wanting to explain to my employees why they might see their benefactor running stark naked into the woods. They'd all get a good laugh, but it was hard to gain back respect after that sort of pale view. Maybe they'd be too absorbed in their coffees and McMuffins to notice?

But when I rounded the back corner of the clubhouse, I found Lucas asleep in a woven hammock he'd strung up beside the back door, a moth-eaten sleeping bag draped over his body. He startled at my footsteps and jerked awake.

"Marty, you've got to let a man sleep in from time to time," Lucas groaned, dragging a hand across his face, scratching the three-day-old beard shading his jaw. He shifted sideways on the hammock and dropped his bare feet to the pine needles below.

"Weren't you just in there?" I asked, pointing over my shoulder to the building's interior.

"Not that I'm aware of. I slept out under the stars last night. It's real life affirming. Have you ever tried it?"

"I mean, I've gone camping, if that's what you're asking?"

"Not the same, but that doesn't matter. What can I do for you?" he asked, pushing his long, thinning hair back into a ponytail with an elastic from his wrist.

"Seriously though? You aren't messing with me? I saw someone in there two seconds ago. They just opened the door and bolted," I said, walking over to the sliding door, which was now closed. I tested the handle, dragging it open and shut, back and forth as if the repetition would illuminate whatever I was missing.

"It's just the plants in there, my friend," Lucas said, brushing the sleeping bag off his lap. He stood, clad in only his boxer briefs, and strode to the door, stepping past me into his crumbling home. "Chock it up to being overworked. You've been getting those plants in the ground at record speeds."

"I don't think—" I began to say, following him inside.

"Don't worry about it, Mart," he cut me off, turning, grabbing my shoulders. He was a little shorter than I was, so the hold was a bit awkward. "Now, what brought you over so early? I know you wouldn't bother me if it wasn't important."

"A whole section's dead," I replied, staring down into his dark brown eyes, unaware if there was a more sensitive way to put it. Death was a weird subject with Lucas. I avoided it whenever I could.

***

They were mostly maples. Sugar maples and silver maples and red maples. All native and hardy. We'd kept up with watering, with making sure there was enough organic compost mixed in with their roots. There was no reason a hundred trees should drop their leaves and rot overnight. They should have been healthy. I'd already nailed a number of museum-quality plaques to their trunks, denoting common and Latin names, a little silver drawing of their leaf structure next to the words. This section of the arboretum was supposed to be stable, established, one of the first we dug in after Lucas gave PlantOrganic the job. But that morning, the short trees looked more like skeletal configurations, white bone cropping out of toxic soil, than the healthy juveniles they had been the day before.

"They said this would happen. It's natural," Lucas said, running a finger along the length of a dead limb, the silver maple snapping in half under his touch.

"Who said what? None of this is normal," I said, taking photos with my smartphone, contemplating the email I'd write to the nursery.

"My friends, the ones who guided me through this whole project. I've mentioned them dozens of times."

"Yeah, yeah, your mystery pals. When are they going to come down and take a look at this themselves?" I asked, gazing out over the valley of dead wood that had once been the seventh hole of Bayside Acres Golf Course.

"Oh, they've been by. A number of times actually. They love what you're doing and think you're a genius."

"Wouldn't it make sense for me to meet them at some point, given they're so involved?" I asked, hating always having some invisible critics to contend with. We need more mulberry down by the sand traps. Weeping willows would be great by the vernal pool. Can't you get larger stock, older specimens, ancient maybe? The answer was always no, you couldn't get older specimens. It was hard enough to get mature trees shipped to the site, let alone any with actual age to their bark.

You can't transplant old growth.

The roots never leave the soil in a healthy transition.

"You will at some point. Trust me. Just have your guys dig these up and replant them. I'll cut you another check."

2.

"Where exactly does he get the money from?" Janelle asked when I got home. She had her jewelry-making tools spread out on the table. Little silver hooks and clasps everywhere, driftwood totems carved into semblances of human faces. She called them Old-Man-Oaks, their beards rough and grainy. She sold them at jam band festivals and psychedelic art shows up and down the New England coast. Cape Cod wasn't exactly the scene for such livelihood, but she didn't mind traveling.

"It's got to be some trust his parents set up before they died," I replied, unlacing my work boots, brushing wood chips and dirt from the cuff. Janelle had all the lights on in our house. She said it made it easier to work. Chandelier bulbs glinted off the marble countertop we installed a few months back, purchased with Lucas's money. The chemical-free organic sofa we'd added to the living room was awash in the bright glow, a fixture that, a year before, had been a torn and tattered leather sofa held together with duct tape we'd inherited from her parents.

Lucas's presence was everywhere in the room.

He was hard to ignore.

"But that much?" Janelle replied, blowing a strand of dirty blonde hair out of her face, adjusting her clear plastic glasses. "He's handed you so much since you started. It's like he's just got a trunk of cash buried in his back yard or something."

"I don't know, Jan. They owned a lot of property. Like acres and acres of it. I try not to ask though. He pays the bills, I pocket my part, I pay my guys, I don't have to search for new clients. It's hard to get anyone to pay on time these days. Don't look a gift horse in the mouth, you know?"

"God, I hate that expression," she replied, standing, wrapping me in a hug, dusting a browned maple leaf from my shoulder. Janelle was taller than I was, almost six feet. One of her arms was etched with a sleeve of mushroom tattoos, the other barren besides the slew of freckles. "Horses freak me out."

"I mean, if they want to fuck your day up, there's not much you can do to stop them. All those muscles," I replied, shivering, thinking about a story I'd read where a woman got her skull caved in from the kick of a mare. "Few things I'd want to fight less than a horse, you know, not that I'm trying to pick fights with animals."

Janelle laughed.

"Are you coming to Scallop Fest this weekend?" she asked, letting me go.

"I don't know. A ton of trees died yesterday and I need to figure out what's up with that. This shouldn't be happening."

"I think most of this shouldn't be happening," Janelle replied, beginning to straighten her jewelry, clearing our table so we could lay out dinner.

"What do you mean?"

Janelle clicked her tongue. "People said they've seen Luke out there in the woods at night, you know, doing weird shit."

I laughed.

"Are we talking about bringing the Salem witch trials back for round two?"

"Talk is talk. I'm just telling you what I hear."

"Hey, I've known him since we were kids. He's always been a bit eccentric. I don't doubt he's out there wandering around at night, but I'm sure he's not like sacrificing babies under the full moon or whatever. He's just lonely. A little sad. A little lost."

"Just because you were friends with someone in high school doesn't mean they're against sacrificing babies."

"Touche."

3.

With a gloved hand, I pressed a finger into the inner cavity of the split hickory, feeling the pulpy innards, rot oozing out like blood from an open wound. The hickory, one of the oldest trees on the golf course, had torn in two, one half crushing a neighboring holly, the other impaling what had once been a putting green on the fourth hole. The entire center had rotted through, with no sign of the illness on the outer bark. Three other trees had met the same fate, rending themselves in the night, crashing down around random sections of the old boundary between forest and manicured landscape.

It hurt my heart.

The old trees were the most beautiful around the acreage.

My guys were taking chainsaws to an oak on the neighboring hole. The harsh rattle of the small engines echoed from the distance, revving high then low, cutting through the quiet bliss that usually infected the fledgling forest. That's where Lucas found me, squatting by the corpse. He looked more awake than anyone ever should, eyes wide, like every cup of coffee in the world swam in his veins. He had his beard shaved off, hair combed, no bags beneath his eyes. The puffy swollenness of his face had been reduced to a youthful veneer.

He stood over me, shadow cast where the tree once stood, feet becoming unseen roots.

"I don't think you can fix this one either," Lucas said, squatting beside me, digging his own bare hand into the black rot.

"I wouldn't touch that. I'm not sure if it's safe for..." I began to say.

"It's fine. It's not like humans catch tree illnesses. We need the old and we need the young, after all. Life from life," Lucas said, examining the black pulp in his hand, holding the dark, jam-like substance up to the sun before wiping it on the grass. "This is kind of like what happened to Mom and Dad, if you look at it in a certain light."

"The rot or the tree?" I asked, not knowing what else to say about the earlier comment. I imagined old growth monstrosities crashing through the roof of a car, cancer gnawing away at bones, but I didn't know if either were even close.

I'd been with Lucas the day his parents died. We were in our senior year, smoking weed in my parents' basement, writing punk songs on instruments his parents bought us. Cal was there on drums. Dan scream-sang whatever lyrics came to him in the moment. We weren't very good, but we had fun, and it felt sort of like family, at least for a while. It wasn't hard to pinpoint the moment the band broke up.

Everything ended with the phone call my mother answered, yelling down into the basement, somehow audible over the distorted chug of Lucas's guitar. He switched off his amp and ran up the stairs. He didn't come back down. We heard the door slam, a car engine growl, then tires fleeing. I asked my mom what happened, but she just cried and cried, saying, "That poor boy," over and over again.

Lucas never told me what happened. The obituary in the newspaper just said they passed unexpectedly in the woods behind their house. The only thing I knew was that they had died together.

Lucas didn't come back to school after that. He disappeared from our lives, which was so startling. He'd always leaned on us, as if some greater sadness lingered in his chest. He was trusting, almost childlike in his attachment to the rest of our friends. Think of a lost fawn, a baby turtle fresh out of its egg at high tide. I gave him a hug at the wake, knelt by the closed caskets, and that was the last time I saw him.

I tried to call.

I showed up at his house.

I frequented the record store and comic shop he loved.

I even asked around with his neighbors, but those were the days before social media, before everyone's footsteps were tracked day and night. It seemed like he vanished, or was in hiding, or the grief had eaten him whole. There had been rumors about sightings of him at the golf course, which had just begun its decline. But there was never any actual proof of his presence.

Not until our phone call a year and a half ago.

"A little bit of both, if I'm being honest," Lucas replied, rising from his crouch. "Some things get crushed. Some things rot from within. It's part of the cycle. Things die so other things might live."

"This is definitely not part of the cycle. You can tell a tree is rotting way before it comes down. This," I said, pointing at the tree, the black weeping wound at its heart, "this isn't natural."

"From rot comes regrowth, right? One tree dies so many more can live. That right there, that's natural. Again, all part of the cycle," Lucas said, eyebrows raised.

"Yeah, sure, but something's fucking with the trees. All those saplings that died yesterday. These old guys today. It's happening too quickly. We were supposed to be finishing up. Now we're going backward."

"Nope. This is all forward, you'll see. Things happen how they need to happen. Just get these dead ones out and keep planting. I think I saw another delivery truck up by the clubhouse. No time to waste."

Then Lucas walked away without further explanation.

It didn't sit right with me.

I only took the job because Lucas had been my friend all those years ago. The first time I'd seen him, on my first visit to the course, he looked withered, as if he'd been drying in the sun like human jerky, all bone and sinew. I didn't know if he had a drug problem, or a drinking problem, or something else, but I had my suspicions. His vulnerability just made me want to help in some way, even if the job seemed ludicrous: convert an old golf course into a massive arboretum. The land would have been worth a fortune if he'd just sold it outright, but Lucas wasn't interested in that. No, he seemed compelled to do the project, like something unspoken depended on it. I had never worked up the nerve to ask exactly what—like I said the day before...gift horse...mouth. And the more trees the better. We'd lost so much of our native forests on the peninsula to deforestation, I was always happy to see some form of restoration underway.

And, like every other ecologically minded landscape designer, golf courses were one of the most glaring sins of the developed world. All those acres cleared for nonnative grasses, all the carbon sequestration shorn at the roots, all those gallons and gallons of water to keep alive what didn't actually want to live here. There was also the issue of fertilizer poisoning ponds and groundwater, but people liked to forget about that whenever they went for a swim or swigged from the tap.

I'll admit, I also enjoyed the fact I was getting to kill one on my own terms, reclaim what had been lost and all that. Lucas and I weren't so different in our desires, it's just that I understood mine. He, on the other hand, hid behind a wall of leaves and branches, never stepping out into the sun.

"Hey, Lucas," I called after him.

He paused mid-step, turning, one hand moving to his shoulder, rubbing at the muscle there.

"Why are we doing this? I think I need to know," I asked.

"Because trees are beautiful and not enough people understand that," Lucas replied with a smile. "Soon they'll understand though."

And then he walked on, explanation a non-explanation.

He passed three of my guys heading my way with their chainsaws and their wheelbarrows. I'd asked Lucas if we could bring in a chipper to take care of the waste, but he said no, insisting we deposit all the rotting wood in a heap in the parking lot. "I've got plans for it," he said. "Don't be wasteful."

He was the boss, so I didn't question—despite the extra work it made for my crew—the illogical reasoning behind it.

Lucas said something to my guys as they neared, something I couldn't make out.

They laughed uncomfortably.

I didn't know if I wanted to hear the joke.

4.

"What weird shit did he say today?" Janelle asked as we walked around the fallow cranberry bog in our neighborhood, our husky, Lurk, striding out in front of us, sniffing patches of wintergreen and wild strawberry. It was our nighttime routine when our schedules aligned, take a walk before sunset while the tree swallows flew low over the bog. She was getting into birding, identifying migratory species that used Cape Cod as a summer residence or a stopover while the seasons changed.

Summer was fading. The chill fingers of fall prodded the air, cooling the sweat that had dried on my skin from the day's long labors.

"Honestly, he mentioned his parents. How they died. I didn't really know what to say," I replied.

"He told you how it happened?" Janelle asked, leaning in, head cocked. "Was it the Mob?"

There had been speculation around town when it happened. Two eccentric millionaires just dying unexpectedly, no information leaked from any source. That was unheard of, especially in a small town like ours. People said it had something to do with smuggling drugs, or art forgery, or some back to the earth utopia cult. There was no evidence to corroborate any of the rumors, but that didn't stop people from whispering about dark dealings that may have never been. I'd even heard they faked their own death for some outrageous life insurance policy. Why bother when you already have that much money just sitting around?

"Not really. He made this vague cryptic allusion to a dead tree I was working on and then he left," I replied, scratching Lurk behind the ears when he brought me a stick. I threw it for him farther up the path, knocking a tuft of dandelion seeds into the air.

"So he's comparing his parents' deaths to the unexpected deaths you're seeing at the golf course?"

"I mean, maybe, but I feel like there's something else there. Something darker."

"I'd buy darker," Janelle said, tossing the stick for Lurk again. She wiped her hand on her jeans, a line of saliva dampening the fabric. "Rachel said he came up to her at the Squire the other night and asked if she'd come back to the woods with him when last call went up. Didn't even offer to buy her a drink."

"You mean go home with him?"

"He said woods. She made it clear that he said woods verbatim. Remember what I said about sacrificing babies the other day? Maybe now's a good time to walk away? He can't take back the money he's already paid you. Things are looking sketchier by the moment."

Janelle was right. We didn't have a formal contract for the work. Just a handshake and a promise between old friends, but things were getting weird. I worried about my guys and all the spreading decay, the vague cryptic words Lucas left me to trouble over at night. But Lucas had been one of my best friends. We'd known each other since elementary school. All the memories of concerts and double dates and stoned evenings were hard to write off, especially after the way we grew apart, that funeral veil cast over senior year.

He was getting stranger with each passing day, but part of me couldn't reason through abandoning our work. Forest restoration was crucial if our ecosystem was ever going to right itself. It was leading by example, showing off a functional alternative to contemporary landscape trends. A few more months and guests could start walking the grounds, seeing the joy of the trees, even though most were still small, what our forests could eventually be if people gave more consideration to conservation.

It wasn't just the money that kept me showing up each morning.

"It's only a few more weeks. A month or two tops. I just want to ride this out and see it through," I replied, as Lurk started to bark at a family of quail that had popped up from the underbrush by the side of the trail. I ran at him and snapped his leash back onto his harness before he decided kibble wasn't a satisfying enough source of protein. He was strong, but I managed to get him to calm down, running a hand through the soft fur on his neck.

"Just promise me when he brings you to his woodland sex dungeon you run in the opposite direction, right? Don't even think about looking at all those kinky vines and shit he's got out there."

I laughed. "Dude would probably mistake poison ivy for Virginia creeper. It's definitely best to skip the itchy bondage."

"Rashes are rarely sexy."

Then Lurk howled, tugging on his leash again. His voice carried across the cranberry bog, startling the swallows that had gathered nearby. They darted back toward the tree line, the air going from a mess of little black and blue bodies to a still tranquility. Chaos to calm in a matter of seconds. Their tiny bodies shivered in the trees all around us, sending a wave of motion from branch to branch until stasis returned.

5.

The voice message said something was in the trees. That something was dying. Another tree? Another section of trees, possibly by the eighteenth hole, possibly the eighth? I wasn't sure. As always, Lucas wasn't the clearest at relaying information. I was starting to doubt he was good with technology, considering the radio silence I received after the initial message. It was after nine, the sun having set an hour ago. The wind brought with it the salt scent of the bay a few miles off, the smell of campfires in the neighboring neighborhood. I parked my dump truck beneath the boughs of an ancient oak looming over the parking lot. A half-dozen gas jugs sloshed around in the dump bed as we came to a stop, left over from the chainsaw work we'd done that morning. I told myself I'd take them out later, that the fumes should be enough to remind me. The pile of rotting wood we'd been stacking took up a number of spaces on the blacktop. It looked like some haunting modernist sculpture catching the streetlight, a thousand arms reaching out from an unseen body, decay creeping along every inch of skin. I was hoping Lucas would just let us burn it, but he said no. It had to stay.

I knocked on the clubhouse door, but no lights were on. All of his potted plants were left in darkness. I listened for footsteps, for the slider at the back of the room to glide open or shut, but nothing stirred.

The eighteenth hole wasn't far. The course looped down and back from the parking lot, the ninth and tenth holes the farthest out, a half-hour walk at minimum if that was the case. But it would only take ten or fifteen minutes to get to the nearer holes in the dark. I went back to my dump truck and grabbed a Maglite.

The flashlight was nearly the length of a baseball bat and had more heft than the wooden alternative. Both illumination and weapon if I needed to smack a coyote or something else stalking the night. There was a pack living somewhere deeper in the woods. I'd never seen them, but their yips dissected the dark from time to time.

I walked down the stone path my guys had installed over the past year, replacing the rutted golf cart track that wound around the property. Bluestone crunched beneath my boots, shifting with each step. I sent Lucas another text while I walked, basically saying where the fuck are you? But with kinder words. Never bite the hand that feeds.

The message went unanswered.

I wasn't surprised.

Passing beneath the original trees of the forest that lined the edge of each once-manicured green, I found myself staring into their crowns.

Lucas had said something was in the trees. I assumed he meant the rot, but maybe it was something else? Something more literal. I hadn't forgotten the shadow I'd seen in Lucas's home. Those thin limbs, the odd movement. If there was something out there, it would be in the old growth, not the new saplings sprouting from the fairway like thin skeletal hands creeping through the lawn.

There was a rustle.

A shower of pine needles descended from above. I swiveled my flashlight beam into the nearest trees, only to greet the glowing eyes of an opossum, its open mouth lined with tiny sharp teeth, three or four infants clinging to its back.

"Sorry, buddy," I replied, dropping the light back to the stones at my feet. "Didn't mean to disrupt family night."

As I spoke, something cut across the path ahead of me. I was too slow with the light, only catching the shivering branches and leaves of the undergrowth where the movement blurred.

"Lucas, if that's you, you really need to get better at answering your phone. This is kind of ridiculous," I said. "The trees look fine."

"But the trees aren't fine," came a voice from the underbrush.

"Lucas, what the hell are you doing?" I asked.

"They will be though. Once you join us. Once everyone joins us."

I shifted the flashlight beam through the underbrush, illuminating winding blackberry brambles and some pointed juvenile holly leaves, but not the body of a man. Just verdant growth and rotting logs.

"Rebirth is what you call it. That is the trade. Rebirth for..."

As the voice spoke, the shadows of the neighboring trees coalesced into the shape of a man, or many men, or one man with far too many limbs to be anatomically a man.

Before whatever it was could finish its sentence, I ran.

Lucas wasn't paying me enough for this shit.

That nightmare shadow was unhinged. A trick of the light? Some odd art installation? Lucas had loved pranks when we were kids, but I wasn't sticking around for the punchline. Clarity wasn't going to make anything better.

I sprinted, breathing hard, the light from the Maglite bouncing over tree bark and skittering across the path. I thought I heard the sounds of another set of feet on the stone, or a dozen sets of feet, but I didn't turn. Nothing good ever comes from turning. I'd watched enough horror movies to know. The parking lot wasn't far away. The streetlight shadows of the oak and the pile of dead wood came into focus, my dump truck just waiting there, a coyote call cutting across the night.

As I made it out from the forest, Lucas stepped into my path, suit-clad, arms reaching around me in a hug surprisingly strong for his size. I dropped the flashlight, its beam shuddering across our feet, casting our silhouettes back into the parking lot. I couldn't break free from Lucas's grip, no matter how hard I thrashed.

"Hey, buddy, what's up with the marathon?" he asked once I stopped struggling.

"Why the hell were you hiding out there? And all that weird shit you were saying. What was that about?" I said, brushing him away.

"I wasn't. I just got back," he replied, pointing to his Audi parked just beyond my dump truck.

"But you said something was dying, like it was serious, like..."

"Oh jeez, I meant I'd noticed another dead tree by the clubhouse. Didn't mean for it to seem urgent," Lucas said, taking out his cellphone, as if he could play the message back for proof.

"Well, it sounded like something was messed up and you needed me here."

Lucas chuckled, putting away his phone. "Well, I'm glad you came running. That means a lot to me. It really proves your devotion to our project. What did it say, if you don't mind me asking? Was the offer good?"

I was taken aback. I wasn't sure I heard him right. Offer? How'd he know there was an offer? Had he heard the voice too? He was way more calm than he should have been and I was really not navigating reality as well as I'd like to.

"Actually, don't worry about it," Lucas said. "I don't want to know. They offer everyone something different. It's personal. Think about it though. I certainly have."

"You realize you sound insane, right? Some weirdo was out there whispering sweet nothings to me and now you're saying I should take them up on it?"

"Something like that," Lucas replied, walking toward the clubhouse, shifting his keys, about to find the right one for the front door.

"I'm not coming to work tomorrow," I yelled after him as he put distance between us.

He stopped and turned, features mostly obscured by the streetlight shadow.

"You know this is bigger than it seems, right? That we need you here. I thought you understood. I thought you were on our side."

"If you aren't going to explain what's up, I'm out," I yelled back.

"You'll change your mind. Think about the offer. Who knows what good can come of it."

Then the lock flipped and he disappeared into the inner darkness of the pro shop. He eventually turned on a light and the room filled with shadowed plants, all those thin limbs, leaves questing for the skylight above. It reminded me of whatever I'd seen in the woods, whatever had talked about rebirth. I shook the thought away, wiping my eyes.

You miss so much in the dark.

Humans weren't meant to be nocturnal.

I had to have overlooked something, I told myself as I got into my dump truck.

But what?

6.

When Janelle's car pulled into the driveway the next day, I left the couch, making sure Lurk didn't sneak out the screen door behind me as he yowled away at her arrival. She'd worked her booth at Scallop Fest all day, listening to the local jam bands riff through vintage speakers, people dressed in *Sesame Street*-esque marine life regalia bouncing through the crowds, everyone drunk, everyone hopefully buying her jewelry. I helped her load that morning, all the totes of hand-carved necklaces and rings, medallions for those who loved astrology, cute little woodland creatures and mushrooms for those who didn't. I wasn't going to make her unload by herself, even though I hoped the boxes would be significantly lighter. Bailing on Lucas's job wasn't going to do our bank account any favors.

I stepped into the driveway beneath the flowering sweetbay trees to find Janelle massaging her knuckles, a blood stain on her light green t-shirt.

"Oh god, what happened?" I asked.

"Your ex-boss wanted to buy some of those tree-man necklaces and then he got a little handsy," Janelle said, walking around to the back of her car, popping the trunk.

"What?" I asked, heat beating beneath my skin. My mind went to the worst places. Lucas was a weirdo, but I never thought he was a creep. There was a distinct difference between the two and I never thought he'd morph from one to the next.

Janelle turned and grabbed me by the shoulders, staring straight into my eyes, sight unblinking. "This. He literally just held me like this for a few seconds over the table, then I punched him in the jaw. He started rambling about needing you back, about how no one else could care for the trees. He was covered in this black tarry stuff, like all over his skin. He looked like a lunatic, like a sick lunatic."

I fished my keys from my pocket and walked toward my truck.

"Where are you going? I still need to unload all of this," Janelle said, gesturing to the totes.

"Lucas needs to know he can't do that. That's fucking assault."

"I think I did more on the assault side of things, if we're being honest," Janelle replied, slamming her trunk shut and running around the other side of my truck.

"I've got this. Just let me go," I replied, Lurk's howls rising from behind our closed front door.

"Nope. Someone needs to get your back. The guy seems unhinged and your right hook has always left something to be desired," she said with a smile.

I couldn't argue with her. I wasn't a fighter.

I hadn't mentioned the dozens of texts Lucas had sent me that morning, all the pleading and begging for my return despite his calm remarks the night before. This time, there was nothing vague about the messages. Something was urgent, something he'd overlooked in the timing. It sounded like his friends had arrived and they weren't happy with the change in plans or acres of dead trees.

He'd always said I would meet them at some point.

I just didn't realize it would be so soon.

7.

The pile of rotting wood was gone, all traces swept from the parking lot besides a few disintegrating scraps of bark tainted black. The sun was fading, long shadows slinking from the old oak at the edge of the blacktop, a number of crows perched in its upper limbs. The temperature dipped, humidity fleeing with summer's end. Lucas always told me to leave the wood, that there was something he needed it for, but in its decaying state, there was little the limbs were good for beyond mulching and adding more nutrients to the soil.

Janelle and I checked the clubhouse, knocking before testing the door handle. The knob turned freely, so we let ourselves into Lucas's home. The scent inside was awful, sweat and compost and turned soil, some sweet tang lingering beneath it all. His plants had been moved to the space beside the sliding door, forming a crowd as if each was about to push their neighbors into the night air, grasping at that last moment of fading sunlight. A number of the ceramic pots were left empty, as if their inhabitants had been plucked up by the roots, spilling soil over the surrounding mess. Odd circular footprints marred the hardwood floors and carpeting, perfectly round, similar to a deer, or a child, or something in between. I called his name, but no one answered. Only a slight breeze drifted through the potted plants, the hint of a word pushed by the wind, nothing articulate, just the moaning of a structure that hadn't been weathertight in years.

"His car's in the parking lot, so he's got to be here somewhere," I said, stepping outside.

"Think he's hiding in the woods again?" Janelle asked as we walked toward the converted cart path. I told her about the thing I'd run into the night before, or the silhouette of the thing, but I fictionalized the encounter a bit, swapping Lucas's arrival with the nightmare, hewing down the number of limbs, the vast reach of their grasping hands reduced to poorly executed shadow puppetry.

"I think he's always hiding in the woods," I replied.

"Metaphorically speaking or literally?"

"A bit of both," I answered.

***

We wandered the arboretum, searching for Lucas, straying from the path here and there to drift into the older surrounding forest. It would have been hard for him to hide in the young growth, their trunks so thin, canopies unestablished. Something had worn a rut down the center of the bluestone path, as if an object had been repeatedly dragged from the parking lot to a distant destination. Scraps of rotting wood flaked here and there like Hansel and Gretel's breadcrumbs, a path we could no longer ignore.

No sense guessing when you possess the map.

***

Janelle and I found Lucas on the sixth hole, a bluff overlooking much of the surrounding forest, its peak almost high enough to see the bay. He was shirtless, smeared with the black decay from the heap of wood he must have been moving since who knew when. What looked like three woven wooden chrysalises stood before us, two that were small and squat, the third the height of a man, a rounded obelisk of sorts, the front unfinished like a giant egg with a hunk of shell removed. Lucas was on his knees before the largest construct, weaving more thin dead branches into the mesh. He startled at our footsteps, eyes swinging to us, then the forest over his shoulder, a smile spreading on his lips. He wore one of Janelle's necklaces, the oaken father image hanging at his throat.

"I knew you wouldn't abandon me. Abandon us." His eyes were on the tree line again, ignoring the hundreds of saplings we'd planted over the last year running down the length of what had once been the fairway.

I tried to see what he was looking at, but it just appeared to be a wall of trees and shrubs in the fading light. Janelle didn't follow my gaze. Her eyes were trained on the smaller cocoons, mouth hanging open slightly, a hand raised over her squinting eyes.

"What's in those?" she asked, pointing at the heaps of wood.

"Mom and Dad. I had to build theirs first," Lucas replied.

My stomach dropped, a sick taste climbing my throat. I hadn't noticed it before, but glimpses of white and sickly yellow peered through the rotting tangle. Knobby bones, femurs and pelvis and tibias, all piled at the bottom of the chrysalis, seen through the holes in the bark like faces on a passing train. There was a skull atop each, only caught in fragments, but unmistakable, eye cavities black and bottomless.

"You dug them up?" I asked, not knowing what else to say.

"Oh, years ago. I had them reburied out behind the clubhouse. It's what they told me to do," Lucas replied.

"They?" Janelle asked.

"My muses. My inspiration. My family. They're the reason we're all here," Lucas said, pointing into the woods. Something stirred there, thin limbs branching from the tree line, trees not quite trees, a body oaken yet fleshy, a face peering out from the pine needles and maple leaves. It seemed to raise an arm in greeting, then a dozen other articulate limbs followed, all dripping sap, all in some state of decay. The whole forest seemed to be awash in life, or half-life, face upon face separating from the crowded greenery.

I stepped in front of Janelle as if I could somehow shield her from what was before us. I left the Maglite in the dump truck. Nothing I had in my pockets was going to protect either of us if those things decided to break from cover. They looked frail, even sickly, but there were so many. I could never fight them all off. I ran scenarios in my head, escape routes, hiding places, but before I could drag Janelle away, Lucas spoke.

"Have you considered their offer? Rebirth? Isn't that what we all want? A new start? A chance to be what we were truly meant to be?" he said, toying with a long stick, the black ichor dripping from his fingers. "I need you to watch our bodies as we change, protect us from those that don't understand, then it will be your turn. You help me with mine, I'll help you with yours once I'm back. I can't finish this myself. You said you wanted to help. You said..."

The things in the woods seemed to nod as much as any tree could nod.

Lucas shook his head, hair matted down with the rot and slick sap.

"You keep planting for us. Keep bringing in new material. Once it dies, build anew. The old are just as necessary as the young," Lucas continued, his voice distant and unfamiliar. "We'll need so many to achieve what they want. It will be beautiful. You'll see. This is just the start. The whole world will understand and change. My parents always told me about the beauty...the honest truth...the restoration of what once was."

Janelle's hand tugged at the hem of my shirt.

"Do you still have those gas jugs in the dump truck?" she whispered without looking away from the rotting chrysalis and the things standing just beyond Lucas, the damp scent of decay growing worse with each passing minute.

"There's a few," I replied.

"I think we need them," Janelle said. "Those are definitely more terrifying than a horse."

"We shouldn't joke right…"

Lucas laughed. "Yes, please, discuss our offer. It's for the both of you. That's what I was trying to say earlier, at your show, but you didn't seem to grasp what I meant. I'm not always the best with words."

"I'm not sure we need to discuss anything," Janelle replied. "We'll help you. We get it. This all makes completely logical sense."

"Wonderful. I knew we were like-minded. I need only a few more minutes and then I will step inside my own. I just need you to finish the last layer. I won't be able to do so from within," Lucas replied. "Someone has to wall me up. My friends don't like to touch their dead brothers."

A shiver passed through the beings gathered in the trees, a wave of revulsion seeping into their limbs.

"Are you sure about this?" I whispered, leaning into Janelle's ear.

"How much gas are we talking about?" she replied.

"Ten, fifteen gallons," I said, picturing all the half-filled jugs crowding the back of the dump truck.

"That will have to be enough," Janelle replied, walking away from my side toward the pile of rotting wood Lucas had heaped around his pods. She bent and picked up a slim sapling that had died earlier that week, carrying it to Lucas. "Just show us how to do it."

"That would be my pleasure," Lucas replied, guiding her hand into the weave, showing her how to slide the branches in place, one after the other like interlocking pieces of a puzzle. She followed his guiding motions as the creatures in the woods watched on, inserting a branch here, tucking a trunk there, roots twisting into one another for stability, the cocoon growing as the creatures nodded along, every inch of the forest swaying in time with the work.

"We'll make sure it's real sturdy for you," I said, kneeling next to Janelle, digging my hands into the rotting wood, black sludge coating my palms as I stuck another branch into the tangled mass. I could practically smell the gasoline, the warm flames engulfing everything before us. Lucas had always been trusting. Of me. Of his new friends. I didn't like to think of how easily he could be taken advantage of, but he was clearly mad, clearly ready to usher in some verdant apocalypse. I couldn't see any other option. I loved trees, but not enough to bow beneath them as they did whatever he said they were going to do.

"Safe as safe can be," I promised as Lucas stepped into the vine-thatched pod, ready for the sky to be obscured, all those dwindling stars cut off by dying timber.

8.

The gas jugs were heavy as we ran across the old golf course, tracing the path we had an hour before, rot-slathered arms growing weary from the sloshing liquid, the acrid scent of petroleum following us with each step. I couldn't keep my eyes from the trees, as if some bark-limbed monstrosity would break from the canopy, gain shape, and drop from the highest branches onto my back. I tried to convince Janelle we should just leave, that we could call the cops and they could deal with it, but she had other ideas.

"They're just going to drag him out of there while those tree-things hide. Then he'll come for us. Or they'll come for us. Whatever, it doesn't matter. You don't just see something like that and walk away without repercussions," Janelle said as we huffed up a hill, making sure not to spill any of our cargo. We'd need every drop. She had a wad of fast-food napkins wedged in her back pocket, a zippo lighter one of my guys left in the truck in her front pocket. A plan doesn't get more straight forward than that.

"We could just get in the truck and drive. Grab Lurk and peace out," I replied, the dread of the coming moment approaching too rapidly.

"This shouldn't be someone else's problem. You heard what he said. This is like a whole planet issue. I love trees as much as the next lady, but not when they're trying to kill me."

"He never said kill."

"What do you think he means by rebirth? You've got to die before you're reborn," Janelle said through gritted teeth, the sixth hole almost in sight.

Beyond the scent of gasoline, that sweet wood-rot reek clung to our skin and clothing. I lost track of how long it took to wall Lucas inside his woven casket. Every stick left a smear of black decay on our palms, catching in our hair from hurried movements. No matter how much you wiped it away, it always seemed to cling in place.

We crested the hill, stepping between recently planted walnut trees and black cherries. The moon cast a silver glow over the three chrysalises, creating the air of religious reverence, some obscene monument to a dying forest god. Inside Lucas's cocoon, a low moan slipped into the night, throaty and distant, somewhere between pain and ecstasy. For a moment, the tree creatures were absent. It was just the pods and Janelle and me and the jugs of gasoline. A forest of just trees. Then there was a high keening and the forest shifted, tree line advancing, each trunk gaining a face and limbs, grasping hands, gnarled fingertips. A thousand emaciated bodies rounded on us, sweeping behind the cocoons as Lucas's moans grew louder.

I didn't know what we were thinking. Pour and burn could never be so simple. Were they just going to let us do it? Just watch from the sidelines? Never. My mind whirred, a chorus of curses slipping out from between my teeth, eyes darting from one approaching oaken form to the next, a wave of wood crashing down around us.

Janelle ripped the cap off one of the gas jugs and threw it into the gathering throng, flashing the lighter with her free hand, flame sparked to life.

"I'll pour the whole thing on him if you don't step the fuck back," she yelled.

The rising mass of leaf and stem and vine halted, frozen, all their near-human eyes looking out at us unblinking.

"That is not something you want to do," a familiar voice said from deep in the crowd. I couldn't quite place the connection, as if I hadn't heard it in years.

"You've got to learn to control your wife, Martin," came another familiar voice, more masculine than the first. "We have a place for you both."

Something pressed through the crowd, the gathered oaken bodies parting, forming a narrow corridor through their depths. After a moment, a hole appeared in their ranks, two thin figures stepping out into the open air. They were shorter than some of their neighbors, a bit hunched, bark cracking around their joints, roots trailing with each step. My heart dropped. The voices were now clear. The faces peering back at me from the thicket were unmistakable, despite the glaze of sap, the open cambria of their skin.

Lucas's parents.

"But your bodies are in there," I said, pointing at the smaller cocoons laden down with unearthed bones. "Wasn't the whole point to bring you back?"

"It's not that kind of rebirth," his mother said. "We had to tell him something to get him to go along with this."

"The boy was never great at asking the right questions," his father said, looking away from us, eyes tracking to the shivering cocoon. "But he did a fine job with all of this. The final step is almost ready."

Then Lucas began to scream, a throat-tearing wail, the sound of trees creaking in the wind echoing from inside the chrysalis as if an entire forest was about to be felled.

"He was always hung up on the bones, but we don't need bones anymore," his mother replied, the screams building, the sounds of flesh tearing, of dry timber snapping in a hurricane. Blood leaked out of the cocoon, running red over decaying wood, pooling on the ground beneath. "He'll understand soon enough."

"It doesn't have to be this way for you though. Some will become us. Some will tend our groves," Lucas's father said, barely audible over his son's screams. "You've been great with the trees. Mother will reward you with a place in her kingdom."

"Mother?" Janelle asked.

"Mother. Everyone knows Mother. And Father, of course. Yes. It is certain. Those carvings you make, the one Lucas wore around his neck. There is no possibility you are unaware of their existence. They have spoken to you all your life. You may not have realized it, but now there is no denying," Lucas's mother said.

"We will all be one soon, our roots intertwined, our minds a single woven mat of mycelium, a being of perfect utopian harmony. Crowns an all-covering canopy. Limbs locked for all—"

Before she could finish, I upended my gas jug, splashing the liquid over Lucas's wood-woven tomb. His screams had become unbearable. I couldn't stand it. This wasn't what he wanted. His parents had practically admitted to tricking him into doing their bidding, and now he was being slowly torn apart in the name of some Mother who had never been his own. He was always so trusting. Always so fragile.

Janelle didn't hesitate. She tore a wad of napkins from her pocket and dragged the lighter's flame across their surface. As the papers began to burn, she tossed them atop the gas-soaked chrysalis. There was a moment of stillness, then the branches erupted into flame. Lucas's screams crescendoed, then fell silent. Only the lap of fire devouring kindling crept into the night. The cocoon went up in a roaring blaze, smoke weeping in thick gouts.

The bark-skinned beings stared at the flames, eyes wide and unseeing. It was like something had been switched off, whatever their brains had become falling into stasis. Then one started to laugh. The rest followed, the sound akin to leaves brushing against one another. A gust of wind swept through their gathered bodies, one creature bending into the next until a hundred rose up together, torsos stuck, roots tangling into one hulking being, a body composed of thousands of bodies, all dripping the black rot that had festered in our planted trees. It had a number of lopsided arms, legs weighed down with trailing roots. I could see Lucas's parents gazing out from the mass, eyes far overhead, looking down as if in pity, as if we couldn't understand the totality of what we'd done.

I snatched the lighter from Janelle's hand, wedged a wad of napkins in the mouth of my remaining jug, and lit the wick. I tossed the plastic-encased molotov as high as I could, but the explosion only crashed about the creature's thigh, a singing squall that receded and died before the rest of the creature could catch. I imagined the black mold igniting like oil, but it only seemed to smother the spread. The creature took a step forward, flattening the burning chrysalis, a storm of sparks climbing from the smoldering heap as it lumbered toward us.

Janelle dropped her remaining jug and we ran.

There were no other options. You can't fight a monster. A god. Whatever that shifting mass of sentient wood had become. It towered over the surrounding forests, putting to shame the fresh growth we'd planted over the past years. Janelle and I wove through the thin saplings, twiglike branches catching our flesh, tearing our skin. I covered my face, crashing through a thicket of mulberry trees my guys had planted too close together. A cut opened over my eye, blood running down, tinting my vision red, feeding copper over my tongue.

Janelle was screaming.

I was screaming.

The whole world seemed to be screaming as we hurried to the bluestone path, the quickest way to the parking lot and the dump truck and our only chance left to flee.

The creature lumbered after us, each step a groaning bellow, dry wood, a thousand leaves shorn in a storm, doorways that hadn't been open in millennia yawning wide. The creature crushed a hundred-year-old elm as it lunged for us, its gnarled hand swiping just over our heads, tearing through the tree's trunk, absorbing the wood, a dangling forearm growing thicker about the wrist.

My lungs burned, my calves and thighs searing like a thousand needles had been shoved into the muscle, separating ligament from bone. Janelle was ahead of me as we made it by hole four and five, climbing out of a valley, the incline not helping anything, trees a blur in our periphery, blood still running down my face, the monster a moon-shot shadow at our backs. I thought it should have been faster, that it should have just swept us up and dropped us into its mouth, but the weak grabs always fell short, each movement inarticulate, like a newborn deer, stumbling on its own legs, trying to learn the boundaries of its fresh, root-thick life.

"Tell me it's unlocked," Janelle called over her shoulder.

"It's unlocked. Definitely unlocked. I wouldn't mess that up," I called back, trying to keep up. Janelle had run track in high school. I was on the sailing team. One of us was more cut out for cardio than the other.

"It's not far. We're going to make it," she heaved.

The singular streetlight in the parking lot glowed like a beacon through the trees, a lighthouse flickering from the distant shore. Stopping wasn't an option. We'd make it to the truck, then we'd drive, putting as many miles between us and that thing as possible. As long as my legs didn't give out. As long as the creature's next grasp didn't catch my shoulder, the hem of my pant leg.

I didn't want to think about that narrative shift.

There was a wheezing coming from overhead, the sound of shallow breath as when one awakened from a nightmare. I couldn't bring myself to look, but I knew it came from the behemoth. The heaviness of the sound, the way it fell on us from above.

Maybe it was dying?

Maybe we'd burned their offering before the sacrifice worked?

No answers came as we sprinted through the last three holes, no longer caring if a tree snagged the flesh of my forearm or calf. My body was just a mass of twitching nerves and adrenaline, pain numbed as my feet began to feel like they belonged to someone else, someone who had been running their entire life, soles perpetually raw and bleeding.

As we climbed the final stretch, rising over the initial hill of the first tee, the parking lot came into focus, the singular light washing over the dump truck, its cab caved in, metal twisted, bed completely flattened by the old oak that had stood over the blacktop. Shards of glass and red plastic headlights coated the painted spaces like a fresh layer of synthetic snow, clotted with the occasional spray of black mold.

"No, no, no..." Janelle repeated, pulling up short by the carcass of the felled tree. A number of the smaller creatures leaned against its trunk, hanging from the upended branches that impaled the vehicle. The windows of the clubhouse had also been shattered, a dull yellow light weeping from within. Not a single pot still held a plant. "We're absolutely fucked."

"Just keep running. We'll take the road. Lose it in the nearest neighborhood," I yelled, turning, heading for the exit.

"I don't think we can lose him," Janelle replied. "He—"

Before she could finish, a guttural below erupted behind us. It sounded like the word *stop* screamed from a thousand lips. In the chorus, a singular familiar note warbled through. My feet failed me and I stumbled, knees going down on the asphalt, tearing my jeans, stone biting into skin, flecks of glass cutting my palms. I rolled on my back to stare up into the creature's face, which undoubtedly had become Lucas's face, his receding hairline and angular cheeks emerging from a weave of vines and roots, pale in the moonlight, wood grain sanded smooth as his mouth opened and closed, testing his new lips.

Janelle stopped farther down the road, screaming at me to get up, to keep running, but then she saw the face, the familiarity, the horror.

"There is no more running," the thousand voices of Lucas said. "Now is the time to weigh options. Some are meant to tend the grove. Others to be consumed by it. Which are you?"

Janelle's hands were on my shoulder, hoisting me up, trying to tug me farther down the road. I didn't budge, anchoring my feet, leaning away. The inevitable had arrived.

"You're right, I don't think there's any escaping this," I said, voice catching in my throat.

"But we can still go, we can..." Janelle said.

"There's trees everywhere. How could we hide? Maybe this is what was meant to happen. I'm good with trees. You heard them. It's a way out."

My words came out in a rattle, slipping past my heaving breath, lungs struggling to recover from the exertion.

"So you're cool with being that thing's servant?" Janelle asked, pointing up at the lumbering behemoth who was now partly my childhood friend.

"Cooler with being its servant than being part of it," I replied, envisioning my skin turned to bark, legs and arms fused into someone else's, enmeshed just below the kneecap, barnacle-stuck, waiting for the next layer of humanity to be woven in place over my body, cutting off all light, the entire world reduced to darkness and the taste of pine sap on my lips, my thoughts only left to the swaying of trees.

When the apocalypse comes knocking and offers you a slightly better apocalypse, you don't turn it down.

Remember, gift horse...mouth.

The monstrous amalgamation of tree and man bent to one knee, bringing his face closer to us, the moon bathing his skin silver, the pinprick of distant stars flickering overhead. The roots or his arms and chest seemed to vibrate, to loosen, as if waiting to reach out and consume, to add a layer of mulch to its spreading garden. Lucas tilted his head.

The countless other heads embedded in his skin turned in unison.

"We'll tend the grove," I called up to him, going back down on my knees.

"Martin, no..." Janelle began before I tugged her down next to me, both of us supplicant to our new god.

"I'm not letting him add you to that," I said, nodding toward the tethered bodies.

Janelle's eyes went wide.

"We'll tend the grove," she replied, tears beginning to flow.

"Good," Lucas replied, hand reaching down, one finger stroking my head as if I were his pet dog. "Plant the young, hew the old."

Then he stood, striding overhead in a single step, roots slithering over the parking lot like a carpet of headless snakes. For a moment, he blotted out the moon with his vine-wrought shoulders, everything falling dark in his shadow. Then he moved on, one lumbering step after the next, heading in the direction of town, a handful of the thin sapling disciples following in his wake, more joining from the woods with each passing moment. I didn't know what would happen outside the grove or what hunger Lucas now possessed, but Janelle and I wouldn't be the ones getting devoured. We'd retrieve Lurk and avoid annihilation, watering hose in hand, pruners sharpened. Anything to avoid consumption, rotting loam filling our mouths, the sap of a thousand dead trees drowning every last breath.

WATERLOGGED

1.

The three story, twelve-unit luxury condominium slid into the sea on the shoulders of a moon tide, kneeling into the waves with the resonance of a ship running aground. It lay on its side, foundation sheared away, windows turned to the cloudless sky.

Glen watched its descent.

It had been his night to search the behemoth of wood and glass for squatters, to trawl the condemned units, kicking out those who lingered in the darkened rooms drinking their lives away or just trying to stay dry.

But Glen's mind wasn't on the bodies that may have been hidden within. He was worried about the creature that swam in the basement, its bone-knit tails and the innumerable mouths that refused to eat the food he left for it. He'd never seen it leave the space, only swimming endless laps as the building grew more and more waterlogged. He doubted it could have escaped in time.

Glen sprinted across the weedy lawn, around plantings gone to seed, and skirted the upturned edge of the building, swinging his flashlight frantically across the ruin, praying for an opening large enough to disgorge the creature he loved like a childhood goldfish, despite its unnatural anatomy, its eyeless face.

At the water's edge, where the retaining wall and rotten decking once stood, Glen found the backdoor to Unit Two crushed into the sand, the boards splintered and stained crimson where the tide couldn't reach.

"Oh god," Glen whispered. He knew the blood could only belong to a single source, but as he drew closer, he spotted something thrashing about through a shattered window and hope flared in his chest.

With a boot blow, the remnants of the door caved inward, and Glen crouched inside. The electricity had been cut years ago. He wasn't afraid of sparks carrying through the water.

On the slanting floor lay a man little older than Glen, a patchy flannel jacket covering his withered frame. He'd fallen between tarnished steel appliances and decapitated chunks of marble countertop. Sheetrock sagged from the walls and flooring from above, piercing the ceiling. The entire building shook with the wind.

Glen thought the man was drunk until he spotted the severed pipe protruding from his chest, pinning him to the wall. Blood was seeping between his lips as he stammered and shook, eyes wide, his arms reaching for Glen, the sound of the ocean sweeping away any sensical syllables.

Glen dialed 911 without thinking, keeping his distance. He'd read that removing an impaled object could lead to further rupture, that the debris might be holding an artery shut. His favorite childhood celebrity had died when he'd been speared through the heart by a stingray. He might have lived if he hadn't removed the barb.

"...what's your emergency?" the voice on the line drawled.

"I'm at three fifteen Beach Street," Glen said, voice shaking. "The condos just fell into the ocean. The condemned ones. There's a guy trapped around back. He's got a pipe through his stomach. I don't know what to do. He's freaking out. I'm freaking—the blood's everywhere."

The words spilled out. Glen tried to slow his speech, to focus, to do something to help the man writhing before him. There had to be CPR techniques, some tourniquet the operator could walk him through. As he stammered into his cellphone, his eyes wouldn't leave the crimson slick draining from the man's chest cavity.

A sense of vertigo swept through his body, the world slipping away beneath his feet as he fell.

2.

"What happened to the body?" a uniformed police officer asked from the end of Glen's hospital bed. The overhead fluorescents were nauseating, the scent of chemical cleaners mixed with the saltwater smell clinging to Glen's skin. He'd been conscious for five minutes, his girlfriend Gina beside him, holding his hand as he recalled what happened in the condos, when the detective appeared, notebook in hand. "You said there was a guy in there. With all that blood, there's no way he just walked out on his own."

The nurse adjusting Glen's saline drip caught her breath, tweaked the plastic piping running down to his elbow, and ducked from the room.

"He wasn't there when you guys found me?" Glen asked, his voice hoarse as if he'd been screaming for hours. He'd assumed the young guy was in a neighboring room, hooked up to bleating machines, artificial lungs pumping his breath.

"No. It was just you and a lot of blood. That sort of thing doesn't look good when you examine it in a certain light," the detective said, eyebrows climbing toward his balding scalp.

"What are you saying?" Gina asked from the side of the bed. Her dyed blonde hair was up in a haphazard bun. She hadn't had time to change out of her pajama pants. One of Glen's winter Carhartt jackets dwarfed her short frame, making her appear more physically intimidating than she actually was.

"Just that we have a murder scene with no body and the only one present was your boyfriend here," the detective said, patting Glen's knee. "The blood's all over the walls. Real unusual splatter pattern. Not consistent with a guy being impaled by a pipe. To tell you the truth, we didn't even find the pipe."

"It was probably the creature in the cellar," Gina said, before Glen could put a hand on her shoulder to coax her back into silence. Images of the creature suspended in a dissection tank surfaced before him, its skin peeled back, muscle exposed on an operating table.

The detective stifled a laugh. "His boss said one of you'd bring that up. But you need proof before you start blaming sea monsters. Anything else you want to add?"

"Nothing without his lawyer present," Gina interjected.

The detective jotted something down in his notebook, laughed, and stepped back from the hospital bed. "You think of anything, you give me a call," he said, flicking a business card between them. It spun through the air and skidded across the linoleum when neither Gina nor Glen reached for it. Then the man was gone, the promise of future meetings hanging in the air like wisps of gun smoke after the cylinder had been emptied.

3.

The pink slip arrived in the mail two days after Glen left the hospital. His boss hadn't bothered to call, to offer an explanation for his expulsion. When Glen dialed the office, no one answered. They had caller ID.

He called his friend PJ instead, another laborer for SeaSide Property Management. They were close, at least as far as coworkers went.

"I heard the owner's trying to dump this on you," PJ said, the sound of wind and sea whistling behind him. Glen knew he was drifting through the vacation rentals in West Dennis, just off the beach.

"Dump what? There's nothing to blame anyone for besides shoddy construction and horrendous land management," Glen replied.

"That's not what they're saying around the office. If someone died in there, the higher-ups aren't going down for it, if you know what I mean."

"I do," Glen sighed, warm anger shifting through his stomach.

He was reclining on a thrift store sofa in the living room of their rented basement apartment, icing his head, which throbbed with the aftereffects of a concussion. Framed posters of classic paintings hung on the walls, making up for the lack of windows, and a grow lamp stood in the corner, keeping a collection of succulents and tiny cacti alive. He'd been watching a documentary on octopus, the creatures crawling in and out of tanks to snatch prey from neighboring labs. Even after one of their tentacles had been severed, it still sought food for the living body.

"I don't know if they're trying to get you on negligence or something, but I'd be careful. They lost a ton of money on that place. Who knows what a murder case would do."

"They can't call it murder when it was an accident. And they don't have a body. How can they have a case if there's no body?" Glen asked, imagining the thickly scaled creature latching onto the dying man's leg, dragging him through the splintered door, its waterlogged bird songs chortling over the fresh kill. If that was the case, they'd never find the remains.

"I don't know, buddy. It's not like I went to law school."

"Just let me know if you hear anything, right?"

"Yeah, no worries," PJ replied, voice cracking through the speaker. "If you need work in the meantime, my uncle's looking for a guy who can throw bricks for his masonry company. You know, when you're feeling up to it."

4.

Gina stood by Glen's side just shy of midnight as high tide crawled around the condo's rotting carcass. Most of the windows had shattered in its descent, glinting shards blinking out from the sand around them. The remaining doors were flung wide, looters sorely disappointed upon realizing that the only thing left in the rooms were veins of mold and tangles of seaweed. Glen didn't want to be there with Gina's old DSLR camera hanging from his neck. She was the one who insisted that if they got a picture of the creature, he'd be exonerated, that the detective who'd been calling for days would disappear, fact dissecting fiction.

She'd bought a ten-thousand-lumen flashlight for the occasion, dragging the beam over the surface of the water, searching for the glint of an eyeless face, row upon row of teeth smiling up from the depths. She'd never outwardly doubted the stories Glen told her, even though the photos he'd shown were grainy at best. If he hadn't deleted them for fear of some technology hack, he'd already be off the hook.

"What's this thing eat?" she asked, turning to where Glen crouched near the building's bulk.

"Besides people, apparently? No idea. It never ate what I left for it," Glen replied. "I must have thrown an entire supermarket's worth of food down those stairs."

Glen tried to stick to the shadows, despite Gina's light. He knew if the police caught him at the scene, it would be another strike against him.

"What if we built a weir out there to trap it? Get all the netting and planks and lines? That could work, right?" she asked, doing another pass with the flashlight.

"Do you know how long it takes to build a weir? Even if we could manage it, that thing is definitely smarter than the bass that get stuck in those things. There's no way..."

"No need to bite my head off," Gina replied, angrily pushing the hair out of her face. "If you've got your heart set on taking the blame for this, be my guest."

5.

Glen sat in a small interview room at the police station, a lawyer he couldn't afford at his side, the blank reflection from a one-way mirror taking up the far wall. The room smelled of stale coffee, and the blue carpet had been worn thin where previous suspects scuffed their feet in nervous repetition. It was the third time Glen had been called for questioning. In each iteration, Detective Bliss, the bald officer from the hospital, made him recite exactly what he'd been doing the night of the condo's collapse. *Now describe this creature for me*, he asked again and again. *So, it's like a bird, a water bird, am I getting that right? With a lot of mouths?* Glen nodded. The image was basically accurate, despite his lawyer's insistence to be vague where the creature was concerned.

"When he asks you about that thing today, just tell him the same thing as last time, alright?" she said, riffling through a yellow notepad. "If you mix things up, he'll get on you."

"But they can't really charge me with anything, right? Not without the body?" The idea had snagged in Glen's mind, that the two correlated innocence.

"They can do a lot with little evidence. It's happened before."

Glen's frustrated reply was cut off by the detective's entrance. A wide smile hung on Bliss's face. It was unnerving.

"We're going to be quick today," Bliss said, sitting on the opposite side of the table. "Either you give us some proof of this sea creature in the next two weeks, or we're slapping you with a murder charge. We can settle everything else in court. I want to avoid all these headaches and the paperwork just like you, but we're not sending our guys on a wild goose chase. Overtime's expensive."

"You can't—" Glen began before his lawyer pressed a palm into his chest.

"Why don't you reign it back in, buddy," the lawyer said. "You need more evidence to start an inquiry. You're rushing."

"The kid's fingerprints are all over everything. The blood from his clothes matches the blood at the crime scene. His boss said he was doing weird things in the building before it collapsed. Something about him handling vagrants more violently than he needed to."

Glen had only thrown one man into the street. The bearded guy had been yelling at the creature for who knew how long before Glen arrived, calling it *Satan Spawn* and *End Bringer* like one of those street corner evangelists. Glen couldn't stand the way the man was treating it like a beast, so he was more aggressive than usual. That was the only time. He had never fired his work pistol, had never taken a swing at the addicts he scared off.

"That's enough of a motive for some judges. Keenness for violence," Bliss said.

"I was only trying to avoid violence," Glen countered.

"You say what you want. Two weeks, and if we don't have some proof, we're taking you in. Don't skip town. We've got you penned as a flight risk."

"My client won't leave. I can assure you of that," the lawyer said, but leaving was the only thing Glen could think about. Borrowing a friend's boat and sailing to Canada was preferable to turning over the creature to those that might do it harm.

But who would watch over the creature if they tossed him in jail? If he wasn't there to protect it?

6.

The company that owned the condominiums also owned a three-hundred-unit assisted-living compound in Hyannis, a golf-side resort in Harwich, and a five-star hotel in Wellfleet. The bad press would lead to more vacancies, more canceled stays, less profits. They had enough money to keep things quiet, to keep the cops from shelling out details to the media. Glen hadn't seen money changing hands, but he could guess what happened behind closed doors. Not a single news article ran in the local papers, no clip of the collapsed building flitted across Channel Five. Glen emailed what he thought were the local papers, only to learn a conglomerate in Florida owned them all, and that no, they didn't care to run his op-ed about the creature. SeaSide Property Management put up a high metal fence around the property to block it off from prying eyes, but it wasn't difficult to sneak behind.

Gina filled the bed of Glen's pickup truck with tuna-grade fishing tackle, a range of casting nets, bloody chum from the local butcher, and every manner of fishing equipment Glen could imagine. He'd told her he couldn't toss a harpoon at the thing, couldn't sling a hook through one of its many lips. He'd go to prison before harming it.

Glen spent countless nights standing at the top of the basement steps, telling the creature his fears and desires, worries he failed to articulate to Gina. There were the wasted dreams of moving away, of getting a marine biology degree to actually protect conservation lands. Water levels were rising. Algal blooms choked shellfish beds. Every year, more and more of his home eroded into the sea. There were projection maps to prove it. He always hoped the creature could help in some way, like a magical fish from myth, granting three wishes when pulled from the deep.

The wishes were slow in coming.

"Don't be a jerk. I went through a lot of trouble to get this stuff," Gina said as she parked the truck in a shadowed lot by the condos. Beach sand blew across their headlights.

"I know, and I appreciate it. But this was the last thing I wanted," Glen said. They were entering week two of the two-week period. The lack of photographic evidence had prodded Gina to look for more extreme solutions.

"I don't want to be doing this either, but you know what I want even less?"

Glen shook his head.

"You in jail. You know this will ruin my life too, right? That it's not just you?"

She was right. They were barely scraping by with her waitress wages and the odd jobs he'd picked up in the wake of being fired. Rent on Cape Cod was outrageous for year-round residents. They'd been trying to save up for a down payment on a house for three years, but their bank accounts were just as empty as they had been at the outset.

"Let's start with the nets if you want to be gentle," Gina said, opening the door.

***

With each cast, Glen and Gina dredged up bait fish and crabs, bladderwrack tangled in the weave. Glen didn't know why Gina was so insistent they'd find the creature in the same place he'd last seen it. He thought it would have made its way to the open ocean, forsaking the shallows for the bottomless deep.

When Gina's arms shook, she ran back to the truck for the surfcaster reels and the bucket of chum.

"I really don't want—" Glen started.

"You don't have much of a choice," Gina interrupted. "We didn't get the photos. If we don't drag this thing in, they're going to pin this on you."

"But we're wasting our time. There's no way it's going to go for the meat. I tried already. Ground beef. Hotdogs. Lamb. Nothing. Maybe it filter feeds?"

"With all this resistance, I'm starting to wonder if you made this shit up," Gina said, hooking a mass of pork, blood dripping down her hand before she let it fly. The pulpy lure sailed across the clouded sky before plunging into the surf.

It took Glen a second to comprehend what she meant. He'd never heard the doubt in her voice before. "Why would I lie? Yeah, it sounds ridiculous, but why would I take that road if I knew people weren't going to believe me? You saw those pictures. There's no denying what was in that basement."

"They were blurry and dark. I thought I saw something down there, but who knows what we were really looking at."

The unseen doubt returned. When he'd shown her the cellphone shots of the creature swimming between the Lally columns in the basement, she'd said it was the most fantastic thing she'd ever seen, like one of those found footage horror movies, but real. She'd even given it a pet name. Burbles, for the sound Glen described to her.

"You never mentioned that before," Glen replied.

"Well, what would you prefer me to say? Yeah, your job sucks and everything about it except this fantasy is soul-crushingly awful?"

"I'm not lying. You have to believe that," Glen said as Gina reeled in the now baitless line.

"I'll believe it when I see it," she replied, skewering another hunk of meat.

7.

"You're cutting it close," Bliss said, standing over Glen in the interrogation room. "I see your lawyer friend's called in sick today."

"She had another client to meet with," Glen lied, refusing to tell the detective he couldn't afford the woman's services anymore, that he'd need to seek out a court-appointed attorney if it came to that.

"Whatever you say," Bliss said, his usual cocky smirk absent. "It's probably better if she isn't around. Everything's basically up to you. I'll be honest—those guys that own the condos, they want this wrapped up quick. We can offer you a plea deal if you tell us what happened to the body. You'll get a shorter sentence. It's the only option I can see working out for you." Glen could feel the detective's pity, suddenly sympathetic for a man he deemed delusional. Glen didn't want the man's kindness.

"I'll think about it," Glen said, standing.

"You've got two days. Who knows, maybe there will be some money waiting for you when you get out. Those guys can be generous."

"Thanks for considering my best interests," Glen said as he stepped past the detective.

Glen never wanted to see the inside of that room again. He wouldn't let Bliss call him back for another bribe, another jab at his sanity.

8.

When Glen got home from the station, he found the apartment in a state of chaos. Kitchen drawers had been gutted, bureaus disemboweled. His clothes were strewn about the bedroom, framed posters stripped from the walls. In all the debris, he didn't find a single item belonging to Gina. Three of their cacti were gone. The flatscreen was missing from its wall mount. Her cosmetics had wandered from their bathroom perch. It didn't take long to find the note stuck to the refrigerator with a magnet that once held a picture of them from senior prom. At least she decided to take it with her, Glen thought as he unfolded the paper.

It was two pages.

Gina let him know of her sympathy, but she couldn't be sucked under with him. She'd worked too hard to see her life eroded by a lie and a ridiculous myth. She'd loved him once but didn't know him anymore. If he had only told the truth, even if he had accidentally killed that guy in the condo, she could have forgiven him, looked past everything. People make mistakes. She knew the kind of guys who hid in the properties Glen inspected. If things got rough, things got rough. They could have spun a self-defense plea, swore the guy carried a knife. Any story was more likely than a sea creature living in the basement.

The end of the note marked the evaporation of eight years of Glen's life. An occasionally anxious but mostly happy time. A hollowness spread through his limbs. Gina had been his high school sweetheart. One of only three girls he'd ever slept with. They'd planned their life together, the family they hoped to start. The Polaroids that Glen had gathered in his mind showing the next thirty years of their shared life burned behind his eyes, the taste of char sour on his tongue.

His phone buzzed in his pocket. It was Bliss. The hours they'd spent inside the interrogation room reciting that same hour of his life again and again was maddening. Glen couldn't shake the thought, the claustrophobia, those words he could never say aloud.

He let the call go to voicemail.

9.

Rocks spilled from the pockets of Glen's work jacket, the night's chilly air working its way beneath his skin. He'd read somewhere that a body remaining in water below fifty degrees would go hypothermic in under half an hour. Nonetheless, Glen took his first step into the surf where the condominium's destroyed deck once stood. The building kept calling him back. When they found his body, he guessed Bliss would apply the same logic he'd considered over the last month. Killer returned to the scene of the crime. No monster, just Glen.

The condo's walls had begun to sink in on themselves, a combination of structural failure and rot coursing through its skeleton. The facade sunk inward, windows and doors and balconies forming a cavern at the building's heart. When Glen pictured the building's demise, it had looked more regal, less like the pitiful lump of mold-pocked timbers behind him.

He was glad Gina wasn't there to see his final decision. Every aspect of his life was moldering beneath his touch.

The water was frigid as it seeped into his boots, rising to his knees. The stones weight was slight, but enough to tip him off balance. They'd offset his natural buoyancy, keeping his feet welded to the ocean floor.

The scent of blood returned to his nostrils, the rivers of red flowing from the impaled man's mouth and gut. Glen didn't know what he could have done to save the guy, what would have alleviated his body's weakness and betrayal, his inability to handle the stress.

It comes for all of us, the man in his memory whispered through rose-hued teeth. Had Glen missed it the first time? He couldn't be sure.

The blear of unconsciousness had wiped all sense of reality from his grasp.

Another few steps and he was up to his chest, pants and t-shirt adhering barnacle-like to his flesh. The weight of the wet fabric combined with the stones was stifling. Gina's words had sewn doubt into his skin, wedged it beneath his ribs, cancerous and throbbing.

But if the creature wasn't real, if it had all been in his mind, what had he been watching those countless hours atop the stairs? What image showed up in those grainy cellphone shots? He was unsure, but he trudged on, water licking at his earlobes, whispering his name in a voice he recognized but couldn't place.

The chill wasn't so bad anymore, the taste of salt inviting, doubt flourishing in his chest, blooming over and over again like the intricate petals of a dahlia.

Then coarse reptilian skin brushed against his open palm.

He yanked his hand away, startled, the sense of touch breaking his fugue, muting his uncertainty. It was too dark to see exactly what swam below, but something was treading circles around his body, appendages skirting his thighs and chest, gently prodding his skin as if greeting an old friend. The rocks in his pockets were heavy, the familiar voice no longer familiar, mocking wishes cast across a great divide.

"I knew...I knew you didn't leave," Glen said through trembling lips.

The creature's eyeless head drifted to the surface, its many mouths opening and closing, tasting the air, tasting his familiarity. Then something small shifted at its side, moonlight catching on another set of fins, another set of mouths, only this time in miniature. Glen had never seen the creature's offspring, had never understood what it had been doing in that basement all those months.

Now he knew.

Glen reached down to stroke the tiny lizard-like snout, scales rough against his fingertips, teeth nipping playfully at his flesh.

Then a boney tail was dragging itself across Glen's back, and he stumbled, water filling his nostrils, choking him as it surged over his head. The weight was too much, the stones pulling him to his knees. The burbled song of waterlogged birds filled his ears, drowning out the crash of waves as they broke against the condo's rotting doorstep.

Like the fallen structure, the ocean had come for Glen—as it would all things in the end.

PUBLICATION CREDITS

"We've Been in Enough Places to Know," *Tiny Nightmares,* Lincoln Michel and Nadxieli Nieto, editors. Catapult, October 2020.

"Mother's Wolves," *Catapult,* July 2021.

"Translations for a Dead Sea," *Metaphorosis,* October 2023.

"Fences and Full Moons," *Flash Fiction Online,* October 2020. (Nominated for a Pushcart Prize and for Ellen Datlow's *Best Horror of the Year* 13.)

"The Tap, Tap, Tap of a Beak," *Three-Lobed Burning Eye,* Issue 34, March 2022.

"The Burnt Floor," *The Florida Review/The Aquifer,* December 2021.

"Wash'ashore Plastics Museum," *Reckoning,* Volume 5, January 2021.

"Growth/Decay" is original to this collection.

"Exoskeletons," *REWIRED: Divergent Perspectives in Horror,* A.R. Ward, editor. Ghost Orchid Press, September 2022.

"Something Aquatic. Something Hungry," *Necessary Fiction,* October 2021.

"Dredging the Bay," is original to this collection.

"Green Thought," *The Southwest Review,* October 2020.

"The Man of Seaweed and Reads," *Humans Are the Problem: A Monster's Anthology*, Michael Cluff and Willow Becker, editors. Weird Little Worlds, LLC, September 2021.

"To Tend a Grove" is original to this collection.

"Waterlogged," *Haven Spec*, September 2022.

ACKNOWLEDGMENTS

I feel like there are so many people that need to be thanked in a short story collection. So many people have been involved with these little guys! I'm deeply indebted to all the amazing editors I worked with on these stories over the years for different magazines and anthologies. So, a huge thank you to: Lincoln Michel, Nadxieli Nieto, Samm Saxby, Sarah Lyn Rogers, B. Morris Allen, Suzanne Vincent, Anna Yeatts, Wendy Nikel, Andrew S. Fuller, Guaraa Shekhar, Elliot Alpert, Jacob Wolff, Cecile Cristofari, Michael J. DeLuca, A.R. Ward, Lacey N. Dunham, Steve Himmer, Tina Albertino, Gabino Iglesias, Willow Becker, Michael Cluff, and Leon Perniciaro. One of the joys of writing short stories is working with wonderful editors. If you get the chance to work with any of the above, don't hesitate!

I also rely on so many great beta readers to make sure I'm not sending junk out into the world. So a huge thanks to K.C. Mead-Brewer, John Chrostek, Rob Costello, Eric Raglin, Sasha Brown, Ali Miller, Robert Nazar Arjoyan, Ben Parson, Mia Baumgarten, Scott J Moses, Thomas Ha, Gordon B. White, and Jonathan Louis Duckworth for making sure these stories (and all the other ones I've sent their way) weren't stinkers :)

As always, a huge thank you to my agent, Marie Lamba, who has championed so much of my weird work over the years and really believed in these stories!

Scarlett R. Algee, my editor at JournalStone, has been such a huge supporter of my writing and has worked tirelessly to get this collection out in the world. For that I will always be grateful!

I need to say possibly the biggest thank you of all to Gabrielle Griffis who really taught me how to hone my writing skills and gave me so much support when I was starting out. I was completely lost and she showed me what a story needed to be...and how to use proper punctuation. That was very important. I wouldn't be the writer I am today without her early nurturing.

A big thank you to John Hennessy for all the guidance during my undergraduate studies. My concrete language wouldn't be the same without you.

An enormous shout out to my mother and father, Kent and Kelly! Mom was always there to read me stories growing up and Dad made sure I never lacked books. They're both wonderful.

I have so many friends who have been there for me over the years, supporting my strange little stories in whatever way they can. So big thanks to Cashel, Daria, Mark, Cori, Rusty, Taraneh, Diane, Stephen, Mia, Natalia, Katie, Ali, Mary-Lou, Tori, Law, Annisha, Jules, Cowan, Kirby, Calvin, Melanie, Mike, Brent, Faith, James, Joe, and anyone else whose name I might have missed (writing acknowledgement pages is stressful! Please forgive me if your name should be here but isn't.).

And lastly, thank you, whoever you are, for picking up my collection. My heart truly lives in short stories. Without you there to read them...where would my heart have left to go?

ABOUT THE AUTHOR

Corey Farrenkopf lives on Cape Cod and works as a librarian. His work has been published in *Nightmare, The Deadlands, Electric Literature, The Southwest Review, Weird Horror Magazine, Bourbon Penn, SmokeLong Quarterly,* and elsewhere. His debut novel, *Living in Cemeteries,* was released from JournalStone in April of 2024. He is the Fiction Editor for *The Cape Cod Poetry Review.* To learn more, follow him on twitter @CoreyFarrenkopf or on the web at CoreyFarrenkopf.com.

www.ingramcontent.com/pod-product-compliance
Lightning Source LLC
Chambersburg PA
CBHW020649260626
47157CB00008B/2967